Escape
from
Memory

MARGARET PETERSON HADDIX

Escape
from
Memory

SIMON PULSE
New York London Toronto Sydney

SIMON PULSE

An imprint of Simon & Schuster Children's Publishing Division

1230 Avenue of the Americas, New York, NY 10020

Copyright © 2003 by Margaret Peterson Haddix

All rights reserved, including the right of reproduction in whole or in part in any form.

SIMON PULSE and colophon are registered trademarks of Simon & Schuster, Inc.

Designed by Ann Zeak

The text of this book was set in Golden Cockerel ITC.

Manufactured in the United States of America

First Simon Pulse edition July 2005

10 9 8 7 6 5 4 3 2 1

The Library of Congress has cataloged the hardcover edition as follows:

Haddix, Margaret Peterson.

Esacpe from memory / Margaret Peterson Haddix.

p. cm.

Summary: Allowing herself to be hypnotized, fifteen-year-old Kira reveals memories of another time and place that may eventually cost her and her mother their lives.

ISBN 0-689-854218 (hc.)

[1. Memory—Fiction. 2. Computers—Fiction. 3. Mothers—Fiction. 4. Kidnapping—Fiction. 5. Cold War—Fiction.] I. Title.

PZ7.H1164 Au 2003

[Fic]—dc21 2002008487

ISBN 1-4169-0338-0 (pbk.)

For my mother and daughter,
Marilee and Meredith

With thanks to my uncle, retired Air Force Command
pilot Jim Greshel, and my cousin, LAPD officer
Karima Tahir, for their assistance
in researching this book. They always gave me wise,
sensible answers, and I appreciated that even when
Kira's story took other twists.

The darkness was coming. I wrapped my arms tighter around Mama's neck and burrowed into her coat.

"Sazahlya," she murmured. "Sazahlya. Molya ste eha dostahna."

Even though I was very little, I could hear the fear in her voice. Something very bad was nearby. That was why she was carrying me through the streets at twilight, a time I normally would have been home in the nursery, curled up on her lap listening to bedtime stories. But I felt safe, because Mama was holding me close. Mama would take care of me.

Lightning and thunder boomed in the distance, a strange kind of lightning and thunder that made me think of toy guns.

Were there guns that weren't toys?

I put my hands over my ears so I couldn't hear.

Mama and I veered through dark alleys and past strange houses. Once, Mama stumbled on a cobblestone, but she threw her arm out and braced herself against a wall so she wouldn't drop me. I cried out with the jolt, and she shushed me: "Shh. Sazahlya, sazahlya, sazahlya."

I buried my face in her neck and was lulled by the restored rhythm of her walking and her reassurances. Sleepily, I decided not to beg for extra bedtime stories when we got home. I tried to tell Mama that, but I couldn't. Maybe I wasn't old enough to talk.

"Ssh," she said again. "Sazahlya."

We turned in front of one of the dark houses. Mama climbed several steep stairs and pulled open a heavy door. Then we were in a small room without any furniture or pictures or even windows. Mama sat on the floor and hugged me, weeping. She rocked me back and forth.

One

I WOKE UP.

"See?" I said as I opened my eyes. "Wasn't that stupid?"

I blinked a few times, so my eyes could readjust to the dim light in the Robertsons' family room.

"So what great buried memory did I come up with?" I asked. "The trauma of second-grade math? I told you it wasn't worth hypnotizing me. My life has been too—" I stopped without saying "dull," because I suddenly realized that all three of my closest friends were staring at me. Their faces, starting with Lynne's thin, dramatic one and ending with Courtney's heavyset, normally placid one, all held identical expressions: eyes wide, eyebrows raised, mouths agape.

"What?" I said. "What'd I say?"

Some thread of memory tickled my brain,

then it was gone. Everything around me was too ordinary and familiar: our sleeping bags spread out on the Berber carpet, the brightly colored bags of Fritos and M&M's we'd been eating before we decided to experiment with hypnosis. It was Friday night, and we were having a sleepover at Lynne's house. That's what we did every Friday night. It didn't fit with the wisp of fear I still felt, without knowing why.

"You never told us," Lynne said slowly, "that you and your mother came here to escape *danger*."

She sounded pleased and intrigued, as if I had presented her with a fascinating physics question. Lynne was the only person in Willistown history who'd ever taken physics as a freshman—or, as Andrea liked to remind her, who'd ever wanted to.

"Or that you had a *nursery* when you were a baby," Courtney said. She emphasized the word "nursery" as though it were something only movie stars and royalty had for their children. Certainly no one in Willistown did.

"Or that you called your mother 'Mama,'" Andrea added.

"Don't all little kids call their mothers 'Mama'? Before they can say 'Mommy'?" I said defensively, though I didn't really know. I was an only child. My friends were the ones with younger brothers and sisters and cousins and—in Andrea's case—

even nieces and nephews. They all had family coming out their ears.

All I had was Mom.

"But you said it with an accent," Lynne said. "And those other words—*Sazahlya? Molya ste eha dostahna?*" She pronounced the words carefully, but her flat Ohio vowels sounded all wrong. "What do they mean?"

"*Sazahlya*'s like 'Hush, hush, it's all right, everything's okay.' People say it to babies," I answered without thinking.

My friends gave me their bug-eyed, dropjawed stares again.

"Not around here, they don't," Lynne said cautiously. "What language is that?"

"I don't know," I admitted.

"Then how do you know what it means?"

"I don't know," I said again. I squirmed a little. The Robertsons' family room, where I'd probably spent half my life, suddenly seemed strange and uncomfortable.

"Then what's that other phrase mean? *Molya ste eha dostahna?*" Lynne asked. She narrowed her eyes, the way she did when a teacher actually managed to find a homework question that was hard enough for her. Courtney and Andrea watched in silence, willing, as usual, to let Lynne speak for them.

Usually I would have been letting her speak for me, too. But now I was trying to shut out the sound of her voice, to hear *Molya ste eha dostahna* the way someone—Mom?—had said it in my memory. I shivered, remembering the cold wind on my face. Remembering hiding my face in my mother's coat.

But that was all I could remember.

I was trying too hard.

"Why does it matter?" I asked. "I probably just read it somewhere. Or heard it on TV. Maybe what you say under hypnosis is like dreaming. Just nonsense."

"But you made it sound so real," Andrea said. It had been her idea to try hypnosis, just because she hadn't liked the video we'd all picked out. I didn't know why I had to be the featured entertainment instead.

I got another flash of memory—the feel of my chubby toddler arms around my mother's neck.

Mom and I did not hug each other.

I sighed. "Tell me everything I said," I asked reluctantly. I resisted the urge to pull my legs toward my body and clutch them with my arms, to huddle like a terrified child.

Why was I scared if it was all just a crazy story I'd made up?

Defiantly, I stretched my legs out and leaned back on my arms—the typical teenager sprawl. A triumph of body language. My fear ebbed. I refused to treat this seriously.

Lynne was already telling my story, word for word, she claimed. Then, of course, she had to analyze it.

"Well, it's pretty clear to me," she said. "You're obviously a refugee from some war-torn country. Your mother must have smuggled you across some border. . . . You moved here when you were two, right?"

"Yeah, from California," I said, rolling my eyes. "No wars there."

"That's what your mother *says*," Lynne countered. "Hey, maybe you're illegal immigrants." Her face brightened, as if she liked that possibility. "Your mother's one clever woman. Who'd look for illegal immigrants in Willistown, Ohio?"

"Every single employer in town," Andrea said, sounding pleased at outsmarting Lynne for once. "You have to show proof of citizenship when you get a job." She was the only one of us so far who had attempted that feat. She was going to be lifeguarding at the town swimming pool as soon as it opened in the summer.

My mother had worked at the town library for the past thirteen years. Maybe thirteen years ago people didn't have to prove their citizenship.

I didn't share this obvious gap in logic with my friends.

Lynne had already moved on to the next puzzle.

"But where are you *really* from?" She squinted at me, as if trying to read some hidden map on my face. "Let's see, thirteen years ago there were battles in Eastern Europe and the old Soviet Union. The Irish-English squabbles were relatively calm"—trust Lynne to carry around a social studies time line in her head—"and there's almost always some conflict in the Middle East and Central America and parts of Africa."

"Do I *look* like I'm from the Middle East? Or Central America? Or Africa?" I asked.

"There are all sorts of people living in all of those places," Lynne retorted. "In fact, that might have been why you had to leave, because the indigenous people threw out the imperialist invaders."

Great. Now I was an imperialist invader.

"You do look kind of different," Courtney offered. "No offense."

I'd been afraid someone would say that. I blushed, knowing that, even with the extra color, my skin was still paler than my friends'. My hair was dark and cut the same way as theirs— longish and pulled back in ponytails or tucked behind my ears most of the time. But in the right light my hair had an almost bluish cast to it. And my eyes were just as dark and ever-so-slightly slanted. Not enough to look Asian. Just enough to look . . . different.

"Then there's your name," Lynne said thoughtfully. "Kira. Kira, Kira, Kira—Slavic, maybe? Russian?"

"That doesn't prove anything," I protested. "Look at, uh, Natasha Jones. Natasha's a Russian name too. Do you think she's an illegal immigrant? A refugee?"

Natasha Jones was a year ahead of us at school and served as the county Beef Queen. She had blond hair and blue eyes, and Lynne had joked once that she looked corn-fed, just like the cattle she promoted. Natasha was Willistown, through and through.

Wasn't I, too?

Andrea reached for a handful of Fritos, as casually as if we were discussing some ridiculous soap opera, not my life.

"You guys are being way too hard on Kira," she said. "You don't have to make her into a foreigner or something." I almost forgave her for the Fritos. Then she went on. "I know what must have happened. Kira's dad must have been an alcoholic or a drug addict or something, and he was always beating up

Kira's mom, so she ran out on him. Disappeared without a trace. Then she hid in Willistown, because he would never look *here*. I saw a TV movie about that once. This woman changed her whole identity and her kid's—your name probably isn't even Kira at all."

Andrea was looking straight at me. I stared straight back. I hoped she thought I was struck speechless by the craziness of her explanation. I hoped she and Lynne and Courtney couldn't tell that if I so much as breathed, I was going to cry.

"Kira's dad is dead," Courtney said. "Isn't he?"

Now she was looking at me too, appealingly.

"Of course that's what Kira's mom would say, to cover up," Andrea said.

I wanted so badly to scream, *Stop it! This isn't a joke!* But I couldn't find my voice.

And didn't I *want* this to be a joke? If it was a joke, it wasn't real.

Lynne's calm, rational voice came as a relief.

"There are lots of things wrong with your explanation," Lynne challenged Andrea. "First, Kira mentioned cobblestone streets and alleys. That doesn't sound like California, where she's supposedly from."

Andrea shrugged.

"It's a big state. I'm sure there's a cobblestone somewhere out there. Anyhow, if you were running away, wouldn't you lie about the place you were running away from?"

Lynne ignored the question. "Two, there's the foreign language Kira was speaking. . . ."

"It's probably just Spanish, and we didn't recognize it. Lots of people speak Spanish in California."

Lynne could have pointed out that all four of us were taking Spanish in school. But we knew Mr. Sutherland, our teacher, had been hired more for his basketball coaching skills than his perfect Spanish accent. He probably wouldn't even recognize real Spanish himself.

Lynne moved on to her next point.

"Three, what about the 'thunder and lightning' that was probably gunfire and bombs?" she asked.

"That doesn't have to be *war*," Andrea said sarcastically. "Maybe Kira's dad was chasing Kira and her mom and shooting at them."

Lynne was clearly losing the argument, but she didn't act like it.

"And third, and most important," she said, "can you honestly picture Kira's mom as an abused woman?"

I could see Andrea struggling with that one.

"Maybe she's changed?" she offered halfheartedly.

Lynne grinned triumphantly.

"Gotcha!" she declared. She turned to me. "So what are you going to do about this, Kira?"

"Do?" I whispered, the best I could do. I tried to remember how to make my voice sound normal, how to make my face look normal. "Why do I have to do anything?"

"Aren't you going to talk to your mom and find out the truth?"

My friends had met my mother, plenty of times. They knew she didn't drive her car, wouldn't touch a computer, wouldn't allow a TV in our apartment. But they'd never really talked to her beyond, "Hello, Mrs. Landon. Is Kira there?" They still seemed to believe that she was like Lynne's mom, who'd given Lynne the menstruation talk a full month before the school nurse brought it up. Or Andrea's mom, who kept better track of who was dating whom at Willistown High School than Andrea did. Or Courtney's mom, who shared dieting tips and hot fudge sundae splurges with her daughter on a regular basis. My friends actually thought my mother was someone you could talk to. Someone you could ask a question.

I forced my hand to reach into the bag of M&M's. I placed three pieces of chocolate on my tongue. I chewed. I swallowed.

"Okay, sure," I said, proud of how steady I managed to keep my voice. "I'll ask."

That wasn't good enough for Lynne.

"But if she tells you none of it's true, will you believe her?"

"Yeah," I said. "My mom doesn't have enough imagination to lie."

None of my friends disagreed.

Two

EVENTUALLY, WE PUT IN THE VIDEO, ONE OF THOSE sappy dramas my friends and I love to cry over. This time, I couldn't even keep track of which character had the fatal disease. Now that I had an excuse to cry, I didn't feel like it anymore.

What would my mother say if I asked her about my supposed memory? Probably, *Such foolishness*, her usual commentary on most matters. I thought of Lynne's question: "Would you believe her?"

It was my memory. Why did I need my mother to tell me whether or not it was true?

I concentrated hard. *Long ago, far away, my mother and me, running away, my mother saying, "Sazahlya, sazahlya"* . . .

Or was it my mother? I could get only flashes of memory, like a videotape that had been partially damaged and badly patched. I couldn't picture "Mama's" face. I could feel the warmth of her arms around me, I could smell her perfume—

My mother doesn't wear perfume.

That was all I needed. The woman who'd carried me, the woman I'd called "Mama"—that wasn't my mother.

Strangely, that made me feel better. The supposed memory I'd found under hypnosis had to be false.

I made myself concentrate on the movie. I made myself eat more M&M's and more Fritos. I laughed when everyone else laughed, but I didn't cry along with the others. I wasn't producing tears for some silly fiction.

In the morning Lynne's dad came in and woke us up with his usual call: "Pancakes, anyone? I'm preparing a feast. If you young ladies sleep any later, we're going to have to call it dinner instead of brunch."

Sleepily, I regarded Mr. Robertson with new eyes. He was middle-aged, balding, just a little bit paunchy. He sold insurance in a little office downtown. Every year he helped Lynne with her science fair project. He was just there, no more noteworthy than the Robertsons' well-worn furniture.

But he was Lynne's father. If Andrea was right, I had one like him somewhere out there.

Or . . . not like him. Mr. Robertson was a nice

guy, if you bothered noticing him. Andrea thought my father was so horrible that my mother and I had had to run away and hide, hundreds and hundreds of miles away.

I thought about everything my mother had ever said about my father. He'd died in a car wreck. He'd worked with computers, which was my mother's excuse for avoiding them. Now that I thought about it, didn't that sound more suspect than romantic?

Then I remembered my mother showing me his picture.

"This doesn't do him justice," my mother had said, holding out a photograph of a dark-haired, laughing man. "He had such vigor, such life. You remind me of him sometimes."

There was an unusual softness in her voice. No one could sound like that talking about someone they hated.

I remembered that I'd decided my memory under hypnosis was all a lie.

But my dreams all night long had been such a jumble. I'd escaped with Mom—no, "Mama," whoever that was—again and again, all night long. Gunfire still echoed in my ears; I could still smell smoke and spices, exotic and familiar, all at once.

Gunfire? Smoke? Spices?

I remembered a movie Lynne had made us all

watch once, about medical students who had their hearts stopped temporarily, just to see what it was like. They all had visions that haunted them horribly and quite dramatically once they were restored to life. They couldn't distinguish anymore between reality and dreams.

Maybe hypnosis did that too.

Why had I agreed to it in the first place? Just because we were bored, and Andrea was insistent, and Lynne said, "Oh, no, you're not messing around with my brain," and Courtney said . . . I didn't even remember what excuse Courtney had given to avoid being the one hypnotized. I noticed we didn't try to hypnotize anyone else but me.

Had my friends suspected I had some unknown memory lurking in my brain? Had I suspected it?

Lynne poked me in the ribs.

"Earth to Kira," she said. "Dad asked you three times if you want bacon or sausage."

I looked around the familiar sunlit room, feeling as if I'd been in a far different place.

"Um, neither," I said. "I'm not very hungry."

"More for me, then," Mr. Robertson said cheerily. I noticed he didn't rush off to the kitchen to finish cooking. He perched on the arm of a chair. "What'd you all do last night after the boring grown-ups went to sleep?"

"We watched this really old movie," Lynne said. "*Dying Young.*"

Mr. Robertson clutched his hand over his heart in mock dramatics.

"Oh, you are so cruel," he said. "I remember when that was just out. Julia Roberts was in it, right? It couldn't have been more than two or three years ago."

Lynne tossed him the video box.

"Check it out," she said. "Early 1990s. Read it and weep."

"I guess your mother and I must have walked five miles each way through blinding snow to go see it," he said. "Or was that how we got to school? I'm so old, I forget stuff like that now."

"Very funny, Dad," Lynne said, yawning. "Oh, yeah, and we hypnotized Kira."

One of the most maddening aspects of having Lynne as a friend was that she told her parents things—just about everything, in fact.

"Did you try to get her to walk like a duck?" Mr. Robertson asked. "Did you convince her she was really a monkey swinging through the jungle? I remember my friends and me trying to hypnotize each other when we were kids, messing around. It never worked."

"Well, it worked on Kira," bigmouthed Lynne

said. "She revealed this really incredible memory about—"

I panicked. I don't know why. Why did it matter what Lynne told her dad?

"Oh, you actually believed me?" I said, too loudly. "I made all that up. Ha-ha!"

Lynne, Courtney, and Andrea gave me stares only slightly less intense than those the night before. Even Mr. Robertson regarded me curiously. The house was so quiet, I could hear the clock ticking in the next room.

Finally, Lynne broke the spell.

"I didn't know you were such a great actress," Lynne said evenly. "Guess you'll be starring in one of these movies someday."

Lynne and I have been friends since kindergarten. She knew me too well.

She knew I had something to hide.

Three

AFTER BRUNCH—WHICH, I'LL ADMIT, WE DIDN'T EAT until one o'clock—parents started arriving to pick us up. At least, Courtney's and Andrea's parents came. Mr. Robertson drove me home.

I sat in the backseat, only half listening to Lynne and Mr. Robertson debate about whose turn it was to mow their yard. I tried to remember when Mom had started assuming other people would drive me around. Everyone else took it for granted. After Courtney and Ashley left this afternoon, none of the Robertsons had said, *Oh, Kira, why don't you call your mom and see what's keeping her?* No, Mr. Robertson had just hollered, "All right, girls, load up the car. Or are famous actresses-to-be too good to carry their own sleeping bags?" The Robertsons were so used to driving me places that I didn't even have to ask. They just showed up in front of my doorstep before school football games and sleep-over nights, before parades and all-county dances.

Meanwhile, my mother had a perfectly good car just sitting in our garage, unused.

I *thought* I could remember riding in that car. I sat beside Mom and couldn't see over the dashboard, even with my car seat making me taller. We drove and drove and drove, cross-country, I guess. I could remember Mom reaching over occasionally to hand me Cheerios and juice boxes. I could remember arriving in Willistown, Mom saying, "Look at that steeple, look at that dome, look at all those Victorian houses. . . ." The word "Victorian" stuck in my brain. It reminded me of something.

Mr. Robertson pulled up in front of our place, one of those Victorians Mom had admired all those years ago. Maple Street is full of them—it's one of Willistown's few claims to fame. The house we live in is a three-story monstrosity, painted pale blue, with turrets and a cupola and frilly gingerbread trim, all the way around the porch. A hundred years ago when it was built, just one family lived here. (Of course, they did have twelve kids.) Now the house is divided up into apartments. Mrs. Steele, who is both our landlady and Mom's boss at the library, has the first floor; Mom and I have the second; and the third has been vacant for as long as I can remember.

"Call me after you talk to your mom," Lynne said.

"Talk to her about what?" I asked, opening the car door.

"You know," Lynne said.

"You two aren't plotting anything, are you?" Mr. Robertson asked.

"Dad!" Lynne protested. "This is private."

"Don't mind me. I'm just the chauffeur," Mr. Robertson said.

"There won't be anything to talk about," I said as I stepped out. I slid my arm through the straps of my sleeping bag and backpack and shut the door firmly behind me.

Stairs lead up the back of the house to our apartment. There's a wide second-story porch at the top—if we wanted to be fancy, we could call it a balcony. When I reached the top of the stairs, I realized that Mom was sitting silently in an old wicker rocking chair on the porch, staring off into space. This was nothing new. Mom watched our backyard the way other people watched TV. And there's nothing *in* our backyard. Grass, a willow tree, a lilac bush that wasn't even in bloom yet. In a month or so there'd be a garden that Mom and Mrs. Steele would plant together, but right now it was early April, and the garden was just a rectangle of dead dirt.

"Hi, Mom," I said.

Mom nodded at me—a greeting that did nothing but acknowledge my existence.

I opened the door to our apartment and shoved my backpack and sleeping bag inside. Then I pulled another wicker chair over beside Mom and sat down.

Mom rewarded me with the ghost of a smile.

If I went along with it, Mom would be delighted to have the two of us sit this way for hours, in silence, regarding the willow tree arcing below us.

I couldn't take it. I looked out at the small wooden garage at the edge of our backyard.

"Mom," I said, "will you let me drive our car when I turn sixteen this summer? After I take driver's ed, I mean."

Mom tilted her head thoughtfully.

"Certainly," she said. "If you have someplace far that you want to go."

There was a lilt to her voice that I'd been hearing all my life. But now I heard it differently. Did my mother have an *accent*? Did she talk the way she talked because she was weird or because she was not speaking her native tongue? Strange, how I'd never wondered that before.

"Will the car even work anymore?" I asked impatiently. "It's been sitting there—what? Ten years? Twelve?"

Mom waved her hands in front of her, just as impatiently.

"It is no matter," she said. "If you need it, it will be there for you."

That's my mom. I'd just wanted to discuss my chance for wheels, and she was turning the conversation into some metaphysical meditation.

No, let's be honest. I didn't just want to discuss my chance for wheels.

I turned and studied my mother's face. She was staring out at the tree again. Her eyes were a dull, ordinary brown—the same color, come to think of it, as the lifeless garden. She had strong features and high cheekbones. One time Andrea had told me, "Hey, maybe that same bone structure will show up in your face when you get older. Lucky you!" But my bone structure wasn't noticeable like my mom's. Mom also had long, thick, steel gray hair, cut with bangs at the front—not the least bit fashionable even in decades-behind-the-times Willistown.

I thought about the debate Andrea and Lynne had had the night before and Lynne's triumphant, "Can you honestly picture Kira's mom as an abused woman?" I had never seen my mother hit another person; I had never seen her so much as disagree with anyone. But everything about her gave off an air of, *Don't mess with me. You'll regret it.*

I sighed.

"Mom, last night at the sleep-over we were goofing off, and Andrea said, 'Why don't we try hypnotizing someone?' And then, somehow, we decided I should be the one, and—"

Mom positively stiffened.

"You were hypnotized? You let yourself be hypnotized? How?"

"With a—" I gulped, caught in the intensity of Mom's stare. "Lynne found this antique pocket watch that had belonged to her great-grandfather. Andrea swung it in front of my face. And then, well, I guess I was in a trance. I remembered something."

"What?" Mom said in a low, urgent voice.

This was the most interest my mother had ever shown in a conversation with me.

"Well, I don't know if it's a real memory," I said. "It was like a dream or something. I was a really little kid and my, um, mama and I were escaping from something bad. We were someplace I'd never been before, and there was danger, and . . . It's not real, is it, Mom?"

Mom didn't answer.

"Mom?" I said again.

Mom seemed to be in a trance herself.

"So it will happen," she said. "Unless . . ."

I thought my mom had her verb tenses confused.

"No, Mom, I want to know if this is something that *did* happen. In the past. Did I—did we—really escape from some other place? Not California?" I was dead certain, suddenly, that the place I'd seen under hypnosis was not California.

Mom seemed to snap out of her trance instantly.

"We came here from California," she said insistently. "That is true. I would not lie to you."

"But before that," I said, remembering the scenarios Lynne had proposed: illegal immigration, war-torn foreign lands, a daring escape across some dangerous border. "Were we from someplace else first? Did I remember something that really happened?"

Mom looked straight into my eyes.

"Put it out of your mind," she said. "Do not think about this again. Do not let yourself be hypnotized again."

"But, Mom . . ."

Mom glanced around fearfully, as if whatever evil we—I?—had escaped from might be lurking in the willow tree. She stood up abruptly and went inside. I followed her.

"Mom, I need to know—"

Mom whirled around.

"No," she spat out. "You do not need to know. You need—I need—for you not to know."

"But I remember—"

"No, you do not remember. Not enough, thank God."

"Enough for what?" I asked, thoroughly puzzled.

Mom scooped up my sleeping bag and dropped it in the laundry room. She slung the strap of my backpack over her shoulder and deposited it on the floor of my bedroom. I wouldn't let myself feel guilty that she was cleaning up my mess. I was on her heels the whole way. Finally, on the threshold of her room, she turned to face me.

"When will you leave me alone?" she asked.

"When you answer my question," I said daringly.

"Then I will have a shadow forever," Mom said with a sad smile. "Because your question is not to be answered." She shook her head. "Kira, you are young. You do not know. You will have to believe me. Some memories are best forgotten."

Her voice was soft, but with an edge to it. I took a step back, and my mother gave me a rueful smile, as if to say, *See? I knew you couldn't handle this.*

Four

I TOLD LYNNE. OF COURSE I TOLD LYNNE. WHEN your best friend is a genius and your mother dumps a puzzle worthy of Einstein in your lap, you'd have to be an idiot not to ask your friend for help.

"I don't get it," Lynne said.

It was Monday afternoon now. We were back in the Robertsons' family room, sprawled at either end of the couch. I had ridden the bus home with Lynne after school, just so I could talk to her in private. Both her parents were still at work. So was Mom, of course, but there was some unwritten law: I went to Lynne's house when we wanted to talk. She came over to my house only when we wanted to study. Sometimes she spent the night when she had a big test coming up the next day. She claimed our apartment had a great atmosphere for thinking—not exactly the reputation I desired.

I picked at a piece of fuzz coming out of the

couch's rough weave. "You're a lot of help," I said, slumping farther into the couch.

"Well, you haven't given me a lot to go on," Lynne said. "Just a bunch of mysterious double-talk from your mom. She really won't say anything else?"

I shook my head.

"And you really don't remember anything else?"

"I've tried," I said. "I racked my brain all week-end. But it's like taking a test—the harder I try to remember, the further away the answer seems."

"Hmm," Lynne said.

"Oh, sorry, I forgot. You never have trouble with answers on tests," I said.

She kicked me gently.

"Shut up! I do so! I know just what you mean. When you're thinking, 'I have to remember the capital of Paraguay, I have to remember the capital of Paraguay,' you don't have a prayer of remember-ing anything. But if you think about something else, the answer just jumps into your mind. Asunción."

"Show off," I said. "I haven't known the capital of Paraguay since fourth grade."

Fourth grade was Mrs. Beltzer's class. I could picture the blue social studies books we'd used, the flag that tilted at the front of the room, the school buses rumbling outside the window. Those details came to me so clearly; it didn't seem fair that the memory I really wanted was so wispy.

"Maybe I should try hypnosis again," I said hesitantly. Mom had forbidden it. But how else was I going to find out any answers?

"I don't know," Lynne said. "I did a little research, and it sounds like it's not something to mess around with." She pointed to a stack of books on the coffee table. I had a feeling they represented every bit of hypnosis research material available at the Willistown Public Library.

"Geez, what are you going to do?" I asked. "Write a report?"

"No, no," Lynne said soothingly. "I was just curious. A lot of that's really flaky. New Age–type stuff. But with serious hypnosis—like what psychiatrists use—there's a lot of controversy about false memories. Like a therapist asks a hypnotized patient about child abuse, and then the patient wakes up convinced that she was molested when she was seven. Even though it's not the least bit true."

"Maybe something like that happened with me," I said. "What did you guys tell me to think?"

I was suddenly angry. Here I'd been agonizing for two days about some stupid memory that my so-called friends had planted in my mind as a big joke.

Except Mom had acted like it was true. And dangerous.

Lynne was shaking her head defensively. Her long brown hair whipped in her eyes.

"All Andrea said was, 'Tell us something we don't know,'" she said. "And then you started talking about darkness and evil. Really, Andrea just wanted to know if you had a crush on John Mizer from your geometry class. She never expected . . . trauma."

I did have a crush on John Mizer—sort of— but there was no way I was going to admit it now.

"That wasn't fair," I said sulkily.

"No," Lynne agreed. "All of these books say it's unethical to try to get information from people under hypnosis without their explicit permission. But we didn't know that Friday night."

I shivered. *Cold. It was so cold in that room with Mama. Waiting.*

"Wait!" I shouted. "I remember—"

"What?" Lynne asked excitedly.

The memory was gone.

"Nothing," I said. "This is hopeless." I slumped back into the couch.

"Not really," Lynne said. She opened a notebook and wrote something in her usual, deliberate cursive. I waited. Then she ripped out the page and handed it to me. "Here's what you need to do."

It was one of Lynne's lists. She's famous for them. I read it aloud.

"'One: Find Kira's birth certificate. Two: Find Kira's mom's birth certificate. Three: Find Kira's parents' marriage certificate. Four: Find immigration and naturalization papers, if any. Five: Find other documents, if necessary. Six: Seek out other living relatives, if any. Seven: Confront Kira's mom with known facts.' Should I read her her rights first?" I asked sarcastically.

Lynne glanced at the list.

"Okay, okay, maybe that last one's a little harsh. I didn't mean it that way. But you deserve to know the truth about your own past."

I could just hear Mom's response if I told her I deserved to know the truth: *Deserve? What does anyone deserve?* She drove me crazy.

I stuffed Lynne's list in my pocket.

Tuesday after school I went straight home, knowing full well that Mom would have to be at the library until at least six. That gave me three hours for detective work.

I started in Mom's room, because I felt guiltiest about snooping there. I wanted to get it over with. She has a bed, a dresser, and a desk. Nothing on the walls, nothing lying out. The first dresser drawer contained a comb and a brush—that's all. The second held a single bottle of hand cream. I closed my

eyes, thinking about drawers in the Robertsons'
house. I'd hung around there enough that Lynne
felt comfortable yelling out from the bathroom,
"Hey, go snag my mom's silver barrette out of her
dresser, will you? It's in the top drawer on the right."
And I'd go and find the barrette in an explosion of
bobby pins and hair clips and old Christmas cards
and bank statements and pictures of other people's
babies. It was the same way in every room of the
Robertsons' house. Finding Scotch tape meant
searching through a kitchen drawer full of Lynne's
old report cards and her older brother's soccer pictures and her mom's grocery store receipts from
the past five years. Every drawer you opened meant
a walk down memory lane, whether you wanted it
or not.

No wonder Lynne thought I'd find my birth
certificate and my parents' marriage certificate
just lying around. The Robertsons had memories.
My mom had a comb and a brush and a single
bottle of hand cream.

I went through the rest of the drawers, but
they were just as bare. Five pairs of underwear and
two bras in one drawer, three T-shirts in another,
two sweatshirts and two sweaters at the bottom.
No envelope crammed with personal papers and
pictures and the past could have been hidden in
any of those drawers.

The desk contained ten pens, eleven pencils, and a ruler. Nothing else.

I thought to look for false bottoms, secret doors, but Mom's furniture was too straightforward: cheaply made, poorly veneered, easily forgotten. It was clearly furniture bought by someone who didn't really care.

I looked under the mattress and behind each drawer, and I was still in and out of Mom's room in ten minutes flat.

The rest of the place wasn't much more challenging. We have sheer, practically see-through curtains on all the windows in the living room, and they seemed to taunt me by blowing around as I searched the couch: *Why are you even trying? Nothing could be hidden here.*

Who was I fooling? I knew every inch of the apartment, from the front door that squeaked to the bathroom window that didn't open all the way to the dent in the kitchen linoleum that I myself had made, dropping a tureen of soup years ago. There were no hiding places.

Still, I was ready to go tear apart even my own room—on the off chance that there was some corner of my own drawers that I'd been overlooking for the past dozen years. Then, searching the kitchen, I reached my hand to the back of a cabinet and closed my fingers around something I didn't know was there: a key. I pulled it out. The hard plastic key chain read, SAFE-DEPOSIT BOX, FIRST BANK OF WILLISTOWN.

Safe-deposit box. Of course. My mom wasn't exactly what you'd call a big-time risk taker. Naturally, she would have placed all of her important papers in a fireproof bank vault.

Especially if she didn't want me to see them.

Five

THE NEXT MORNING BEFORE I LEFT FOR SCHOOL, I tucked the safe-deposit box key in my pocket. I'm not sure exactly what I wanted to do. I figured Lynne could come up with a plan.

I packed my own lunch and yelled at Mom's closed bedroom door, "I'm leaving now! Bye!" Mom had the day off, to make up for working Sunday. So she wasn't even up yet. I didn't wait around for a response.

I was one of the few kids at Willistown High who could walk to school. It's ten blocks. A bus would stop for me if I stood on the corner and looked pitiful when it was raining or snowing or just plain cold. I'm sure that all the other walkers had parents who would drive them during bad weather, so the bus drivers really went out of their way to be nice to me.

But this was a pleasant spring day, almost

warm already. I took off walking on my own.

I thought again about my mother's virtually empty drawers, her refusal to go anywhere she couldn't walk, her strange silences and cryptic replies. She really was an unusual person. I just took her oddities for granted—and so did everyone else in Willistown. Small towns have the reputation of expecting everyone to be the same, but in Willistown people seemed to protect my mom in all her peculiarities. My mom's boss, Mrs. Steele, probably should have fired my mom when all the library's records were computerized—what kind of a librarian won't touch a keyboard, can't look up any computerized reference source, can't even answer the question "Is this book checked out already?" without walking over to the shelf to look? Even though she'd kept her title and salary, I didn't see how Mom could be anything but a glorified clerk now—good for nothing but shelving books. Yet Mrs. Steele always raved about Mom, her knowledge of books, her encyclopedic recall of obscure details, her patience and speed in helping patrons.

Why wouldn't she help me?

A new thought struck me: Maybe Mrs. Steele was nice to Mom because she knew Mom's secret. Maybe the whole town knew except me. Maybe even Lynne was just playing along. . . .

Boy, I was really getting paranoid now.

I reached the end of the block and crossed the street to pass Miller's Drug Store. Miller's Drug Store is an anachronism—one of those old-fashioned drugstores that every small town had fifty or sixty years ago and practically no town has now. At least, that's what the articles in the *Columbus Dispatch, Cleveland Plain Dealer, Cincinnati Enquirer,* and *Dayton Daily News* said. Mr. Miller has them all lined up in the window, yellowing in the sun. I heard someone ask him once what it was like to be famous, and he said, "You know, it's funny. Thirty years ago everyone was making fun of me because I didn't get rid of my old cash register, didn't replace perfectly good display cases, was just plain too lazy to change. That's what they said. Now people drive here from all over the state and write me up in those big-city papers. . . . It's a strange world."

This morning Mr. Miller was outside scrubbing his plate-glass windows.

"Hi, Kira," he said as I walked past. "Need any chocolate to make it through the day?"

"No, thanks, Mr. Miller," I said. I looked past him, through spotless windows, to the famous Miller's Drug Store candy counter. He had jelly beans, gummy bears, Necco wafers, gumdrops, malted milk balls, chocolate stars, M&M's, and a dozen other candies all lined up in glass cases, right at a kid's eye level. When I was little, that candy counter seemed like the eighth wonder of the world.

"Well, if you do, don't forget who taught you all about it," Mr. Miller said with a chuckle. "I can still remember you coming in with your mom, pointing at the Milk Duds, and saying, 'What's that?' I couldn't believe it, a kid not knowing candy. I don't see how people can stand it, all that health food out in California."

Mr. Miller had told me this story a thousand times—probably every time I'd seen him over the past decade. I knew his words by heart. Next he was going to remind me how he'd taught me not to bother with the pointless candies, like Smarties and circus peanuts, and go straight for the good stuff: chocolate. Then he was going to rail again about my "wacky California child-hood" without candy.

But suddenly I froze, hearing the familiar tale with new ears.

Mom had never once complained about Mr. Miller giving me candy. If she'd opposed it in California, why hadn't she opposed it here?

Maybe because we hadn't come from California. California wasn't so foreign that they didn't have Milk Duds.

"Mr. Miller," I said slowly, "when you gave me candy for the first time, you could tell I'd never ever had it before, right?"

"Oh, yeah," Mr. Miller said, laughing. "You should have seen your face. Wish I'd had a camera that day."

"Okay. Thanks," I said, thinking hard.

Mr. Miller was still shaking his head, savoring the memory. I turned the corner, veering away from my usual path to school.

The bank was three blocks away, right across from the county courthouse. In fact, with its marble pillars and limestone facade, it's what most people notice instead of the county courthouse.

Of course, at seven thirty in the morning, the bank was closed and deserted. I stood across the street, staring. Somewhere, behind those thick walls, hidden away in a vault, there had to be answers to all the questions growing in my mind. I fingered the key in my pocket, wishing.

Six

LYNNE PUNCHED NUMBERS INTO THE CELL PHONE.

"Yes, I'm thinking of opening a safe-deposit box with your bank," she said into the phone, faking a sophisticated voice. "And I was hoping you could answer a few questions?"

I stood like a guard beside her. We were hiding out in the second-floor bathroom at school. We'd gotten special permission to come up here because Lynne had told Mrs. Grayson, the teacher on cafeteria duty, that the nearest bathroom was too crowded and we really had to go. Mrs. Grayson hadn't even blinked. It pays to hang out with straight-A Lynne—teachers never think that good students are going to do something bad.

Never mind that students aren't supposed to be making personal calls during the day. Students aren't even supposed to be carrying cell phones. But Lynne's parents had gotten her one right after those shootings at that school in Colorado, and Lynne dutifully carried it everywhere. Other kids might have used it all the time, racking up calls to all their friends. But this was the first time I'd seen Lynne even pull hers out of her backpack.

"Mm-hmm, mm-hmm," Lynne said. "And how much does that cost each month?"

I dug my elbow into her side, made a face, and moved my hand in a circle. She knew I meant, *Come on, get on with it. Ask what we really want to know.*

Lynne made a face too and turned her back to me.

"Yes, I see. That does sound inexpensive," she said. "I was also curious about your security measures. How could I be sure that no one else would have access to my box?"

Lynne waited. I pressed close, trying to hear, but the bank teller's voice was barely a buzz. Lynne shook her head at me and mouthed, *Tell you later.*

"Okay. Uh-huh. Hmm," she said. I hoped Lynne was remembering whatever the woman was telling her, instead of focusing all her attention on coming up with different responses.

"No, I think you've told me everything I need to know," Lynne said. "Thank you very much."

She shoved down the phone's antenna and looked at me doubtfully.

"How good are you at impersonating your

mother and forging her signature?" she asked. "And how willing are you to go to jail if you're caught?"

I shook my head.

"It's hopeless," I said. "Everyone in town knows my mom."

"Well, she does kind of stand out," Lynne said apologetically.

We trudged back to the cafeteria. I spent the rest of lunch period explaining to Andrea and Courtney why I wasn't going to storm into the bank demanding to see the documents that were—at least in Andrea's and Courtney's minds—rightfully mine. Or, alternately, why I wasn't going to force, trick, or bribe my mom into telling me everything.

"But mothers are so easy," Andrea argued. "Just act interested in their pitiful little pasts, and in no time at all they're telling you everything. The name of their high school prom date. The first movie they saw with a boy. How badly Uncle Jake flunked calculus. The only challenge is staying awake for it all."

"That's your mom. Not mine," I said, even as Lynne said to Andrea, with great interest, "Your uncle Jake flunked calculus? Isn't he the one who's a math professor now?"

I sighed and stared over my friends' heads. I

wished I'd never told them anything. I couldn't take back what I'd said under hypnosis, but I could have pretended I'd just made it all up. That way, maybe I could have forgotten it too. I could only imagine what horrible secret Mom was hiding from me: Rape? Murder? Abuse? Alcoholism? Violence? War? What other bogeymen were out there? But discovering the truth could not possibly be worse than this half knowing, this half suspecting.

I barely spoke to my friends the rest of the day. Walking home, I was conscious at every point of how far away I was from the bank. I went two blocks out of my way just so I didn't have to walk past Mr. Miller's store again. But I was steeling myself.

I had never demanded anything of my mother in my entire life. But today I was going to demand that she tell me the truth. I didn't know which of Andrea's recommended methods I was going to use. I didn't know if I'd be forced to make up an approach of my own.

But whatever I did, it was going to work.

Seven

MY HEART WAS POUNDING BY THE TIME I REACHED the top of our stairs. I'd never felt so daring. I unlocked the door, banged it open, and yelled out a challenge: "Mom!"

She didn't answer.

I walked through the kitchen, the dining nook, the living room. I looked in the bathroom, both bedrooms.

Mom was nowhere in sight.

How dare she, I thought.

She had probably just walked to the grocery, or even to Miller's Drug Store, to pick up something totally boring, like toothpaste. I might have run into her if I'd taken my usual way home. Rationally, I knew I shouldn't take her absence personally.

But I was still furious.

Trying to calm down, I walked back through

the apartment. This time, I saw that one of the chairs at the dining table was turned on its side. I'd probably knocked it over myself, in my haste, and hadn't even noticed.

That sobered me a bit. I bent down to put the chair back right.

But down low, I had a different perspective. I could see something silver glinting on the floor, half hidden by carpet fibers. I reached for it. As soon as my fingers closed around it, I knew what it was. A key.

This one had no key ring attached, no label explaining its use. I turned it over in my hand and saw the initials "GM." General Motors.

This was the key to Mom's car.

I kept turning the key over and over, automatically, as if I'd eventually turn up an explanation. Why was the key here? Probably it had just fallen out of Mom's pocket. But why would she have been carrying around the key to a car she hadn't touched in more than a decade?

I tried to remember if I'd seen this key the day before, when I'd been searching for my birth certificate. Mom had so few possessions, you would have thought I could have noticed that one was missing. But my mind came up blank.

Honestly, I was a little spooked, finding the key on the floor by an overturned chair. (*Had* I knocked it over? Or had it been like that when I came home? I couldn't remember.)

Holding the key tight, I felt around on the floor, just in case Mom had dropped something else. Our carpet is deep green and thick—it's easy to lose things in it. But all I found were crumbs from the English muffin I'd eaten for breakfast. That was a little odd; usually Mom vacuumed on her day off. *She must have been lazy today,* I thought scornfully. *Too busy keeping secrets to do any work.*

That was the attitude I needed to hold on to if I ever had a prayer of confronting her.

I straightened up and slid Mom's key into my pocket. So I had the safe-deposit box key on my right side and the car key on my left, both held tightly in place by the material of my jeans. Maybe I could hold my mother's keys hostage until she told me the secrets they might unlock.

I really wanted Mom to hurry up and come home. I wasn't going to be able to stay mad at her much longer. Soon I was going to start worrying.

Resolutely, I forced myself to sit down at the kitchen table and pull out my history homework. *Name three causes of the American Civil War and . . .* War? Did I remember a war?

I kept having to read the history questions over three or four times. It took me a full hour to write ten answers.

And at the end of the hour Mom still hadn't come back.

This was really weird. Mom wasn't the kind of person who always left a note whenever she went out. But she also wasn't the kind of person who was ever gone long.

I called the library. Mrs. Steele answered the phone.

"My mom isn't there, is she?" I asked. "You didn't call her in to work at the last minute, did you?"

"No." Mrs. Steele sounded surprised. "Goodness knows we're busy enough this afternoon—how many term papers are your classmates trying to do? But I couldn't call her in to work during a leave of absence. The public employee code prevents it."

"Leave of absence?" I asked, certain I'd misunderstood.

"Yes, yes. I still can't believe the library board approved her request so quickly. She didn't say— Are you two going to be out of town? Is she taking you out of school for that long?" Mrs. Steele was often frustrated with my mom's closemouthedness and tried to get information out of me instead. Sometimes I played along, sometimes I didn't. Right now, I was even more baffled than Mrs. Steele. And, in her nosiness, she seemed to have forgotten I thought my mom was at the library. "No, it's five cents a day for overdue books," she added.

"What?" I said.

"Sorry, Kira," Mrs. Steele said. "I was talking to somebody else. Wish I were taking a month off too. Oops—gotta go. No! Do not pull all those books off the—"

I hung up, thoroughly confused. Why would my mother take a leave of absence? For a whole month? And why hadn't she told me? Why wasn't she home? Could she possibly have left town? Without me?

I picked up the phone and automatically began dialing Lynne's number. I didn't even have to look, I've dialed it so many times. But this time, I stopped halfway through. What good would it do to tell Lynne what was going on? Mom would probably walk in, just as I was saying, *Yes, my mom is definitely weird*. That wouldn't exactly set the right tone for Mom to reveal all.

And I suddenly wasn't sure I wanted Lynne to know the latest developments. Mom was weird, all right, but it was the kind of weird you could live with and not have to pay too much attention to. Ever since I'd been hypnotized, the weirdness had spread. Lynne was beginning to treat me like a particularly perplexing math problem, not a friend. I wasn't going to encourage that.

I did the rest of my homework with unusual attention to detail. I even did an English assignment that wasn't due until Friday. When I finished, it was practically six o'clock, and Mom still wasn't home.

I stood up, stretched, walked around the table. I really wished we had a TV. All my friends always had something to do, a way to kill time whenever they wanted. Turn on the tube, flip through all the channels a time or two, and, zap, there went that half hour you didn't know what to do with. There went those thoughts you didn't want to think, replaced by clever talking frogs, housewives delighted with their clean laundry, rock stars revealing their love lives, Oprah frowning empathetically over some sad tale.

I picked up a book—Mom's favored replacement for TV—but I couldn't concentrate. I considered fixing dinner, because I was getting hungry. But I didn't want Mom to think I was rewarding her for being away. No, let her fix dinner, for her and me both, as soon as she got back. Let her pay for scaring me.

Just to do *something*, I settled for vacuuming, because I was getting sick of stepping on crumbs every time I walked around the table. I hauled out the sweeper and swiped it across the floor under and around the table. Bored, I pressed on, over by the wall, over toward the door. Something jammed in the bottom and rattled, vibrating against all that suction. Irritated, I kept going, but the rattling continued.

"Okay, okay," I muttered, and switched off the vacuum.

It was a small scrap of paper stuck against the turning belt. I yanked it out. I don't know what made me bother looking at it. But once I looked, I stared.

On the paper, in such a messy scrawl that I barely recognized it as Mom's writing, were the words, *Take the car. Go to Lynne's.*

Eight

I DIDN'T DO IT. I DISOBEYED.

I mean, really. I'm only fifteen. I don't have a license. I'm not sure I've ever even touched a steering wheel. And Lynne lives way over on the other side of town, practically out in the country.

Besides, after a decade, who's to say the car would even start?

I could have called Lynne and asked her parents to pick me up. They would have come immediately.

But this was too weird. If Mom wanted me to go to Lynne's, why hadn't she told me in person? Why hadn't she left a clear note where I was sure to see it? Why hadn't she told me she was taking a leave of absence from work? Why hadn't she explained my memory to me? Why wasn't she here?

I brooded. At seven o'clock I finally got up

and made myself a peanut butter and jelly sandwich, because I was going light-headed with hunger. (I wanted to blame hunger.)

By seven thirty I was staring out the window at the dusk . . . and then the darkness. My brain didn't seem to be working very well. I'd think, *I should call someone,* but I wouldn't move. It was too hard figuring out whom to call, what to say. I was fifteen, not some little kid. I didn't need my mother waiting for me every day after school. Let's say I called the cops and reported my mom as a missing person. They'd laugh me off the phone. *She's only been gone a couple hours?* they'd say. *And you're worried? Are you sure she didn't tell you she was going someplace, and you just weren't paying attention?* (Had she told me she was going someplace, and I just hadn't paid attention?)

My mother never went anywhere.

My mother also never took leaves of absence from work. She barely even took vacations.

Something was really, really wrong. And I couldn't begin to figure out what, based on the scanty clues I had: the note, the key, the overturned chair. (*Had* it been overturned before I walked in?)

The phone rang, and I jumped three inches, panic coursing throughout my body. I grabbed the receiver.

"Hello?"

"Hey, Kira. Are the science fair entry forms due this Friday or next Friday?"

It was Lynne.

"Um, I don't know. I left that folder at school," I managed to say.

"You okay?" Lynne asked. "You sound kind of strange."

That was my opening, my chance. I could spill all to Lynne, and she—or her parents—could reassure me, comfort me. Find my mom.

"I'm fine," I said.

Suddenly I remembered reading about how little kids trapped in house fires tend to do everything wrong: Rather than rushing to a door or a window, their natural instincts tell them to hide in the closet or under the bed. Hide where you can't see the fire, and maybe it won't be there.

I was doing the same thing. As long as I didn't tell Lynne that something was really, really wrong, it was all in my head. Paranoia.

". . . get my dad to drive me over to the library, then," Lynne was saying. "Want to meet me there?"

"Huh?" I struggled to make sense of Lynne's words. It was like my brain wasn't capable of understanding. "No, thanks. Not tonight," I finally said.

I hung up the phone and just stood there staring at it for a long time. When I turned around, a strange woman was standing in the doorway of the kitchen.

"Who are you? What are you doing here? Where's my mother?" I asked, my questions tumbling out rapid-fire. I wasn't scared—that is, no more scared than I'd been for the past few hours.

The woman regarded me silently for a few seconds. She chose to answer only one of my questions.

"I," she said, "am your Aunt Memory."

Nine

THE WOMAN SPOKE THOSE WORDS—"I AM YOUR Aunt Memory"—the way someone might say, *I am the president of the United States* or *I am the queen of England.* She clearly expected me to understand immediately, maybe even to curtsy or bow.

When I did none of those, only stared blankly, the woman gasped.

"She didn't explain?" the woman asked incredulously. "She never told you?"

"Who? Told me what?" I asked. Some calm, reasonable part of my mind was thinking, *Pick up the phone again and call the police! Now you have a reason!* But I hesitated, studying the woman. She had dark hair, pulled back from her face. She wore a long, flowing dark coat, of some sort of wool, too heavy for April. I judged her to be in her thirties or forties. About my mom's age, maybe older. She didn't seem to be a threat. She wasn't aiming a gun or a knife at me.

She seemed more like a clue. A better one than a key or a scrap of paper.

"You mean my mom," I said. "You mean my mom never explained."

"I mean Sophia," the woman said. And in her pronunciation of my mom's name I heard the same, faint accent my mom had. An accent I'd been hearing my whole life without knowing it.

"Then you explain," I said, and was instantly amazed by my own boldness.

"There is no time now," the woman said, glancing impatiently over her shoulder. "You must come with me."

This had gone too far. I placed my hand back on the phone, ready to knock the receiver off the hook. I could punch in 9-1-1 without looking, behind my back. I would, if the woman so much as took one step in my direction.

But what if the police came before I got any answers?

"I can't go anywhere right now," I said cautiously. "I'm waiting for my mom to come home."

The woman gave me the kind of pitying look our teachers give the stupidest kids at school. Part *I don't have time for this right now,* part *I can't believe how dumb you are,* and part *I feel really, really sorry for you, not being able to do any better than that. What will ever become of you?* It made me feel about three years old and dumber than a dog.

"Sophia," the woman said, "is not your mother."

I could see her mouth moving, but I'm not sure I heard her words. Rather, I felt them, deep in my heart, deep in my brain.

I waited for the jolt of shock. It didn't come. Somehow I had known this—for how long? Since my hypnotized memory of escaping with "Mama," at least. But probably longer than that. I called my mother "Mom." I put her name down on all those forms we had to fill out for school. I'd given her a Mother's Day card every year. I loved her, I guess. But there had always been something at the back of my mind, I thought now, some inkling that went beyond wanting my mother to be more like my friends' mothers.

"Why did she say she was?" I asked weakly. My grip on the phone slipped. It didn't matter.

The woman shrugged. She was watching me carefully.

"She kidnapped you," the woman said. Her accent seemed even more pronounced suddenly. "Do not judge her too harshly. I believe she thought she was protecting you. Crythe then was . . . dangerous."

"Crythe?" I asked numbly.

The woman no longer seemed surprised by my ignorance.

"Crythe," she repeated. "Your home. Where Sophia is imprisoned now. She has been kidnapped now too. You must come and save her."

Ten

LATER I WOULD WONDER WHY I BELIEVED HER SO quickly. I wasn't stupid. I wasn't naive. I'd heard the same "stranger danger" lectures everyone gets, from preschool on up. I wasn't sure I trusted this woman. But she claimed to be my Aunt Memory, whatever that meant, and memory was exactly what I was starved for.

Plus, she seemed so sure that I would believe.

"Quickly now," she said. "Pack a suitcase."

"I don't have one," I said. Apart from overnights at my friends' houses, I'd never gone anywhere that required packing.

"Ah," the woman said, almost approvingly. "Some other container?"

"I'll use my mom's," I said. "Sophia's."

I dragged out the big, black suitcase that had sat in the hall closet as long as we'd lived there. I'd searched it only the day before.

While the woman watched, I carried it into my room and lay it down on my bed. I went to get my toothbrush and toothpaste. It seemed surreal to care about dental hygiene at a time like this. But I was grateful to have insignificant details to focus on.

"Is it cold there?" I asked as I walked back into my room. "And how many days should I plan on?"

"These should be enough," the woman said, holding up a stack of jeans, sweatshirts, and underwear.

She'd gotten into my drawers. While I was in the bathroom, she'd gone through my clothes, made her own selections.

"Um, thanks for helping, but I like to keep my possessions private," I said, taking the clothes out of her hands.

The woman blinked. Her eyes were the color of rainwater, clear and undecipherable.

"But I'm your *aunt*," she said. "Your Aunt Memory. I am supposed to know everything about you."

"Oh," I said. I stuffed the clothes in the case. Alarm bells were going off in my head. "Things must be really different in Crythe than they are here, because . . ." I looked at the woman again. She had her head tilted to the side, studying me as carefully as if she were about to face a test. About

Kira Landon: Which of her top front teeth sticks out, ever so slightly? Which side does she part her hair on? Which eyebrow is thicker?

The woman was giving me the heebie-jeebies. I didn't finish my sentence.

"Well, let's go," I said in a too-loud voice. I was suddenly eager to leave, before I chickened out. Before I came to my senses.

"Do I make you uncomfortable?" the woman asked. "I forget you have not been raised in Crythe."

"A little information about the place would help," I grumbled, zipping the suitcase. The woman picked it up.

"I'll tell you in the car," she said.

That was the incentive I needed. I turned off the lights in my room and then in the rest of the apartment. I grabbed my jacket, locked the door, and put the key in my jacket pocket.

Three keys, I thought strangely. *I have three keys now.*

My heart pounded unnaturally as I followed the woman down the dark stairs. There was still time to turn around, to run away, to find someone else to listen to the woman's story. Someone who wouldn't be blinded by hope and fear, as I was.

I stopped at the bottom of the stairs. I had a sudden flash of memory: I had waited in this very spot, my first day of kindergarten. And then Mom had come down the stairs and walked with me to school.

"You're not scared, are you, Kira?" Mr. Miller had asked as we passed his drugstore that August morning, so long ago.

"No," I had said confidently. Then I leaned in to whisper, "But I think my mom is."

Mr. Miller had gotten a big chuckle out of that, treated the whole thing like a joke. I'd heard him afterward, repeating my words to other customers. Otherwise, I would have forgotten. But now I could remember the white, stretched look of Mom's face on my very first day of school. She had been scared. She'd been terrified, and not just because her little girl was growing up.

"Is my mom— Is Sophia—," I said now. "Is she in great danger?"

"I will not lie to you," the woman said. "Yes. She is. But it is not too late. You can save her."

How could I refuse?

But I remembered Mom wasn't really my mother. I remembered she had kidnapped me. I didn't move.

The woman kept walking until she reached a strange car parked in the driveway by the bushes. She opened the trunk and shoved my suitcase inside. Then she turned around and noticed I was hanging back.

"Kira?" she said. "Come on. We've got to hurry."

"Um," I said indecisively. This was all too strange. I didn't know what to do.

"Kira?" the woman repeated. She left the trunk open and walked back toward me. I saw the shadowy bushes beside the car moving in the breeze. I stared at them, wanting the shadows to give me a sign: Go or stay.

"I see what is needed," the woman said as she reached my side. She put her arm around my shoulder—to comfort me, I thought.

Then I inhaled a sharp, sweet scent, and I forgot everything.

Eleven

AN ENGINE HUMMED. I WAS ALMOST WAKING UP, almost winning the fight against sleep that kept trying to pull me back in. My head throbbed in time with the noise. With my eyes still shut, I tried to remember where I was. That humming engine, all the vibrations . . . Was I on the bus, riding to school? How could I have fallen asleep on a ten-block bus ride? My brain wasn't alert enough for logic.

I let myself slip back into sleep, into a dream. I was on a bus. In my mind I could see the dream bus, empty except for the driver and me. I stared at the back of the driver's head, many seats ahead, and it seemed like the driver must be my mom. I thought I should recognize her. But how many times had I looked that closely at the back of my mother's head? Then the driver turned her head and looked back at me, and it wasn't Mom at all. It was that strange woman, Aunt Memory.

Then I was truly awake. Groggily, I opened my eyes and looked out the window my forehead was pressed against. Instead of the familiar streets of Willistown, I saw only clouds, dark and far below me.

I wasn't on the bus at all. I wasn't even in a car. I was on a plane.

I jerked back from the window so quickly, I hit my head on the back of the seat.

"Wha— Where—" I couldn't form a complete thought, let alone express one.

Aunt Memory turned around in the seat in front of me.

"You're awake now," she said calmly. "How do you feel? Are you hungry? Thirsty?"

I stared at her. How could she ask such normal questions when we were who-knew-where and I had no memory of getting there?

I ignored her questions and looked around, wildly. The plane was a small one. Aunt Memory sat in the front beside a man I assumed was the pilot. It was too dark to see him clearly, but he looked old, wizened, and nearly bald beneath his headphones. The instrument panel glowed in front of him.

My seat, behind them, was smaller and less

padded than theirs. My suitcase was wedged in beside me. I put my hand on it, as if the feel of a familiar object could reassure me.

I noticed that Aunt Memory and the pilot had no luggage.

"You said you'd explain everything in the car," I accused Aunt Memory. "You didn't say anything about a plane!"

I saw Aunt Memory's shoulders rise and fall, carelessly.

"You were hesitant enough as it was," she said. Somehow her accent seemed more pronounced than ever. I could barely understand her. "I saw no reason to frighten you."

"*Frighten* me?" I fumed. "You don't think it's frightening to be knocked out and then to wake up in an airplane going to—Where are we going?"

"Crythe, of course," Aunt Memory said impatiently. "Just like I told you. Crythe is far away, and our arrival there is urgently awaited. You didn't think we had time to drive, did you?"

"I didn't have time to think," I grumbled. "I was too busy being"—the right word came to me all at once—"kidnapped. You kidnapped me!"

I glanced at the pilot, wondering if he'd heard me. Weren't pilots bound by some sort of international law by which they were required to report crimes? Unless, of course, Aunt Memory had a gun shoved in his side and was hijacking him, as well as kidnapping me. Or unless he was her accomplice, as committed to the kidnapping as she was.

All of this suddenly seemed too silly to be believed. I wasn't the sort of person who got kidnapped. I didn't think I knew anyone who was the sort to get kidnapped. And yet, if Aunt Memory's story was true, I'd now been kidnapped twice, and Mom kidnapped once. Ridiculous. We weren't celebrities or millionaires or princesses of endangered countries....

Were we?

Aunt Memory had turned around completely now, and she was looking me directly in the eye. Even in the near darkness, I could make out sympathy in her gaze. I couldn't think of her as a kidnapper.

"Kira, I *am* sorry," she said. "I know this must be very . . . distressing for you. I wish there had been a better way. I assure you, I mean you no harm. How could I? I'm your Aunt Memory."

Once again, she said those two words reverently, as if "Aunt Memory" were gold coins she was handing me to treasure forever.

"But what does that mean?" I asked sulkily. Refusing the treasure. "Do I have an Uncle Memory, too?"

Aunt Memory laughed, and even over the rattle of the plane engine, her laughter sounded musical.

"Oh, no," she said. "Aunt Memory is not my name. It's my, um, title. In Crythe every child who is born has an Aunt Memory. A special female— usually a relative, sometimes a friend of the mother—who is charged with teaching the child everything there is to know about being Crythian."

"So which were you?" I asked. Rudely.

"Pardon?" Aunt Memory said, sounding more foreign again.

"A relative or a friend? Did you know my"—I swallowed hard—"my real mother well? And my father?"

I was willing to back into the subject of my real parents, my fake mother, my kidnapping. I wanted to know everything, but I was scared to hear anything. It was like having a scar that hurt to touch. I just couldn't help reaching for it.

"Yes," Aunt Memory said softly. "I knew your parents well."

Her voice was as gentle as memory itself. I forgot I'd asked another question too.

Twelve

"YOUR MOTHER WAS SO BEAUTIFUL," AUNT MEMORY said in a dreamy voice. I leaned forward to hear better over the engine noise. "And brilliant, too, like your father. . . . And so talented. When either one of them walked into a room, it was like the lights were suddenly brighter, the colors more vivid. Everything glowed. They had charm— 'charisma,' I think it is called in English. They were like—like the glorious flames that moths are attracted to. Everyone was a moth compared with them."

I thought of poor, mousy, mothlike Mom— the woman I'd assumed was my mother all these years. No one could accuse her of having charisma. Or talent or brilliance. But she did have a presence. People noticed her, too.

It was strange that I felt such a stab of loyalty to Mom suddenly. I was willing to believe that she wasn't my real mother. I was almost willing to believe that she'd kidnapped me. But I still felt like defending her, to myself, if not to Aunt Memory.

"What did they do?" I asked Aunt Memory.

"Do?" she echoed.

"What were my parents' jobs? Their occupations?" I was testing her. If she didn't tell me that my father worked with computers, it would mean—what? That Aunt Memory was lying? Or that Mom-who-wasn't-my-real-mother had lied more than once?

"Um . . ." Aunt Memory seemed to be searching for the right words. "I think in English it is called 'instructor.' No—it was more than that. 'Leaders'?"

"They were in charge of Crythe?" I asked in disbelief.

"Yes and no." Aunt Memory tilted her head thoughtfully. "It is hard to explain. We in Crythe rule ourselves. We do not have kings, presidents, chancellors, premiers. Not like outside. But there are some who . . . stand out. Like your parents."

A new thought struck me.

"But they died a long time ago, right?" I asked, suddenly unsure. Aunt Memory didn't sound like someone discussing long-dead friends. Her voice was raw, and I thought I saw tears glinting in her eyes. She looked like someone at a funeral, grieving the newly deceased.

Aunt Memory winced at my bluntness.

"They both died in the war," she murmured.

War, I thought. I imagined Lynne saying, *I told you so.* It was my turn to wince.

"There was a war in Crythe," I said flatly. "When I was—what? A baby? A toddler? What were they fighting about?"

"The same thing they are fighting about now," she said. "The cause you will help us with."

Cause? What cause? I wondered if I'd misunderstood. But before I could ask any more questions, the pilot suddenly spoke up for the very first time.

"Sahmoleyna blizo," he said.

Aunt Memory answered him in a flow of foreign words. Crythian, I assumed. It sounded amazingly familiar, but I didn't have the slightest idea what she said. It was like hearing a song I'd memorized years ago and then forgotten. Now I couldn't pick out any of the notes.

Aunt Memory turned back to me.

"We are landing now," she said. "You have your seat belt on, yes?"

I nodded, watching what I could see of the pilot's face. He showed no sign of understanding Aunt Memory's English words. So I could not appeal to him with, *Oh, please, I don't understand what's going on!* I had no one to help me at all.

I peered out the window, but there was only darkness. Then I saw two thin rows of lights on the ground, far below. Wherever we were landing had to be an incredibly small airport, far from any city. I'd never flown before, but surely I should have been able to see streetlights and houses, office buildings and highways. Here there was nothing but one runway.

"Where *is* Crythe?" I asked. "Have we flown over water? What continent are we on?" I was so disoriented, I didn't know if I'd been unconscious for minutes or hours or days.

From the front seat, Aunt Memory chuckled.

"You would say," she told me without turning around, "that Crythe is in California."

Thirteen

THEN WE WERE ON THE GROUND. I HAD NOTHING TO compare it with, of course, but the landing seemed awfully rough. Were we supposed to bounce at the end of the runway?

Aunt Memory and the pilot said nothing, simply unfolded themselves from their seats and climbed out. Aunt Memory held the door for me.

With the plane engine shut off, the vast silence around us seemed to echo in my ears. I peered past the runway lights. We were on the edge of some sort of woods. I thought vaguely about running away, but there was nowhere to go.

"My car is over there," Aunt Memory said, pointing out into the darkness.

"*Nya mesta*," the pilot said behind us. He was struggling to pull my suitcase from the plane.

"*Sah, sah*," Aunt Memory said, and laughed. She explained to me, "Jacques is joking that your suitcase is heavy. Before, when he was putting it on the plane, he asked if we'd packed bricks. Look at what a good actor he is."

The pilot had the suitcase out now and was pretending to strain to carry it over to Aunt Memory's car. I knew the suitcase could barely have weighed five pounds; it was like watching a supremely talented mime.

"*Mozheh teh li auto*," the pilot grunted.

"*Det skudu! Makhahy teh seh!*" Aunt Memory said. Though I didn't recognize any of her words, I understood her tone. *Enough clowning around,* she was saying. *We don't have time for this.*

Aunt Memory turned her back on the pilot and stalked to the car, parked in grass just beyond the last runway light. I watched the pilot for a moment longer. He still struggled with the suitcase, though his movements were less exaggerated.

Maybe he wasn't such a great actor. Maybe he was just very weak. Or maybe there was more in the suitcase than I thought?

Aunt Memory opened the passenger side door for me and the trunk for my suitcase. Neither one of us could see the pilot put it in. He slammed the trunk, and Aunt Memory started the car.

"He's not coming with us?" I asked hesitantly, not wanting Aunt Memory to hear the fear in my voice. Why did I think I would be any safer with the pilot along?

"No. Jacques must see to his plane," Aunt Memory said.

We were going up a dirt road now. I had the impression that we were in the mountains. The headlights shone on nothing but more trees, more rutted road. The car shook with every bump we went over. I'm not exactly up on my car brands, but this one was the kind that high school students barely scraped together enough money to buy. The seat was vinyl, the dashboard unadorned. I doubted that it had any shock absorbers. If my life had depended on guessing the car's make, I'd have given a *Jeopardy!*-style answer: *What's the cheapest car made in the past twenty years?*

Maybe my life does depend on knowing a detail like that, I thought distantly. *I'm in real jeopardy. I'm being kidnapped. I need to stay alert.*

But it was hard to think that way. I didn't want to believe that Aunt Memory was dangerous. I wanted to believe that she was showing me my past, helping me save my mom.

We kept on driving into darkness.

"What—" I cleared my throat. "What exactly am I supposed to do to rescue Mo—Sophia?" I asked.

"Why, denounce the kidnappers. Appeal to all of Crythe for her release," Aunt Memory said.

"That will work?" I said doubtfully.

"Of course," Aunt Memory said. "In Crythe just the sight of you, your parents' daughter—you have power."

I puzzled over that one. I was supposed to have power? I'd never felt so powerless in my entire life. Fear clutched my stomach. What if I did something wrong? What would happen to Mom? What would happen to me?

"I'm supposed to make an appeal on TV?" I asked tentatively. "Couldn't you have just filmed me back home and—"

"On TV?" Aunt Memory said sharply, interrupting. "No. Of course not. Not in Crythe. You will speak in the town square. To everyone."

Aunt Memory acted like "TV" was a bad word. Why should that surprise me? Mom's hatred of television had to come from somewhere. Maybe all Crythians disapproved of it. Maybe Crythe was one of those strange cults you hear about, left over from the 1960s.

I had trouble picturing Mom as a cult member.

"You still haven't told me very much about Crythe," I said in a small voice.

"We'll be there soon," Aunt Memory said.

I waited for her to say more, but she didn't. She kept her eyes on the road, driving with an intensity that seemed familiar. Who else drove with her fingers clutched so tightly around the steering wheel, with her back ramrod straight, her mouth clenched shut, her eyelids barely daring to blink? Then I remembered: Mom did, or had, back when she actually drove.

I shut my own eyes, trying to conjure up the image of Mom driving. If I could see something of Mom in Aunt Memory, or Aunt Memory in Mom, then I'd have another clue. Proof, maybe, that Mom really had come from Crythe (and therefore I had, as well?).

The next thing I knew, the car was stopping and I was straining to wake up from another deep, confused sleep.

"Here we are," Aunt Memory said.

I opened my eyes and stared.

Fourteen

WE WERE PARKED BEFORE A STONE CASTLE, WITH rows of stone houses stretching up and down the street beside it. Some of the houses had thatched roofs and red window boxes spilling over with geraniums.

Old World, I thought. *We aren't in California. We're in . . . Slovakia, maybe, or Ukraine. Or some ancient village in Greece.*

I hadn't been to any of those places, only seen pictures in my social studies books all throughout school. Maybe streets in Slovakia, Ukraine, and Greece have McDonald's golden arches glowing on practically every corner, just like in the United States. Maybe the pictures I'd seen were carefully edited for my schoolbooks, to make us think the Old World still looked old. But Crythe was those pictures come to life. I almost giggled, remembering how I'd imagined it as some leftover 1960s cult.

Now I expected to see girls in kerchiefs and peasant skirts, boys in knickers. Heidi and Peter the goatherd, eating goat cheese and home-baked bread.

While I'd been gaping, Aunt Memory had circled the car. Now she opened the door for me. I stepped out on uneven cobblestones.

Cobblestones.

Suddenly Crythe didn't seem so charming and fairy tale-like. This was a real place. This was where my mother had carried me from danger, all those years ago, where the woman I called "Mom" had kidnapped me. And where I was supposed to be speaking about a cause I knew nothing of.

"I'll wake a servant to get your suitcase," Aunt Memory said.

Her voice echoed on the silent street. There were no other cars in sight. But I was almost relieved to notice that the old-fashioned-looking streetlights actually glowed with electric bulbs.

Aunt Memory was reaching for the stylized latch on the castle's imposing front door before her words registered in my mind. I jerked to attention.

"Uh, no," I said quickly. "It's late. There's no need to disturb anyone. I can carry my own suitcase."

I didn't want anyone else complaining about

it being heavy, making Aunt Memory suspicious. And if I carried it, maybe I could figure out what else was in it besides the clothes I'd packed.

Shrugging, Aunt Memory stepped back to the car and opened the trunk.

I reached in and tugged. Fortunately, the way the trunk was designed, I didn't have to lift the suitcase up, just straight out and down.

It was heavy. It was as heavy as the eighty-pound bag of water-softener salt Mrs. Steele had once asked if I could carry down to the basement for her. I couldn't.

At least I could drag the suitcase, and I did. It went *bounce-thump, bounce-thump, bounce-thump,* all the way to the castle door. I was glad there wasn't a curb and sidewalk—the street went right up to the castle wall.

And I was glad that Aunt Memory was occupied with opening the door, not watching me.

As soon as she had the door open, two men in uniform stepped out. They both wore black pants and fitted gray jackets. I couldn't decide if they were military uniforms or servant uniforms.

"Oh!" Aunt Memory said, sounding surprised. She spoke quickly to the two in Crythian, her voice so low that I caught only scattered words. Then she turned to me.

"They'll put your suitcase in your room. We'll

go to the kitchen for a snack. And I think it's time for me to explain everything."

"Past time," I muttered under my breath, so low nobody could hear. But I was all too happy to surrender my suitcase to the men and follow Aunt Memory into the castle.

Fifteen

THE CASTLE HAD A GRAND, ECHOEY FOYER, WITH formal, stone-floored rooms on each side. But as I followed Aunt Memory, we quickly reached cozier rooms. The kitchen itself wasn't any bigger than the Robertsons' back home. I sat at the table, and Aunt Memory heated water to make tea. Incongruously, she used a microwave, not a kettle.

"So you have microwaves, just not TVs," I said, trying to be provocative.

"Some Crythians have TV," Aunt Memory said. "The younger ones. But it is hard for the rest of us."

Hard? What was hard about TV?

Aunt Memory brought two mugs of tea to the table. She sat down.

"You need to know the history of Crythe first," she said. "Most Crythian children can recite the *Book of Crythe* by age five. But it is not your fault that you are so far behind."

I waited, ignoring the hint of insult.

"Crythe is an ancient civilization, founded by Romans before the fall of the empire," Aunt Memory began, stirring her tea.

"Romans came here? To America?" I asked incredulously.

"Allow me to finish," Aunt Memory said frostily. She stared into the hot tea, obviously in no hurry to go on. Minutes passed before she looked up. "There is a ... ritual for telling this story. It is to be the first thing any Crythian can remember. But it is wrong in English. And your brain is already ... occupied? Is that the right word?"

I shrugged. "Can't you just tell it the best you can?"

I was surprised to see tears in Aunt Memory's eyes.

"But it is sacred...."

"So Romans settled Crythe," I prompted, suddenly terrified that Aunt Memory might shut off the explanation. I couldn't really believe that the Roman Empire had anything to do with Mom's kidnapping—or my own. But I had to keep Aunt Memory talking.

"Yes," Aunt Memory said. "Outside Crythe,

most people have forgotten what the Romans excelled at."

"Building aqueducts?" I guessed wildly. "Fighting wars?"

"No, none of that," Aunt Memory said impatiently. "Remembering."

I stared at her blankly.

"Paper was scarce, and they had a complex society. The petty bureaucrats would memorize tax documents. Their poets could recite long epics by memory. They schooled their children in methods of memory almost entirely forgotten in modern times. And in the supreme act of memory, in 447 B.C., the orator Simonides remembered all two hundred and forty-one guests at a dinner party after they were killed by a falling ceiling. He'd been at the party earlier, then stepped out briefly. When he returned, everyone was dead, crushed beyond recognition. But he identified them. Think if they had died unknown."

They were dead either way, I wanted to say. I didn't dare. Aunt Memory was clearly crazy. She had a strange glint in her eye all of a sudden.

"This is your memory, your heritage, your past," she chanted. She nudged my arm and hissed, "Say it after me!"

"This is your—," I began.

Aunt Memory frantically shook her head. "This is *my*—" she prompted.

Halfheartedly, I repeated, "This is my memory, my—what was it? My heritage. My past."

Aunt Memory frowned but went on.

"And in Crythe the heritage was not forgotten. We are what we remember. We do not forget," she said, still in that hushed, reverent voice.

I was out of patience.

"So you remember the Romans?" I asked. "That's what makes Crythe special?"

"No, we remember everything," Aunt Memory said. "What we had for breakfast on our fifth birthdays. Every book we've ever read. Every conversation we've ever had. Every person we've ever met. Everything."

"Yeah, right," I said, more rude than I normally would have been. She was even crazier than I thought. "Sure you do. What was the first thing I said to you?"

"You said, 'Who are you? What are you doing here? Where's my mother?' Then I said, 'I am your Aunt Memory.' Then you said nothing, and I said, 'She didn't explain? She never told you?' And you said, 'Who? Told me what?' And then, 'You mean my mom. You mean my mom never explained.' And I said, 'I mean Sophia.' And you said—"

"All right! All right!" I interrupted. Aunt Memory even had my inflections down. It was like listening to a tape. I blushed. "But that was just a couple of hours ago. Even I remember most of that."

"September, the year you were born," Aunt Memory continued smoothly, "I met your mother and father on the street, and they were showing you off. 'Best baby ever,' your father said. And your mother apologized: 'Don't mind Alexei. Every father has to think that.' And your father said, 'But I'm the only father who's right. Kira is the best baby in the entire history of the world. And I should know, because I'm the one who had to memorize all those genealogy charts.' And, Kira, you were an awfully cute baby. You had on a pink eyelet dress and a little bonnet edged in white lace, with a satin ribbon under your chin. And you were cooing."

Aunt Memory could have been making it all up. I wouldn't have known the difference. But it sounded so real. . . . I wanted to believe that my parents had thought I was the best baby ever.

It was my turn to have tears stinging at the corners of my eyes. I tried to stay logical.

"How?" I asked. "How do you remember everything?"

"We train ourselves—our Aunt Memories

train us. We pay attention," Aunt Memory said. "And we avoid that which we do not want to remember. We do not clutter up our minds with nonsense."

No watching TV, I thought. *No surfing the Internet. And does driving a car count as nonsense?*

How could I have lived with Mom for more than a dozen years without her ever telling me she remembered everything that had ever happened to her?

Did she remember everything?

"Mom—Sophia—she can do that too?" I asked.

"She could," Aunt Memory said. "Before. Everyone in Crythe could."

Before? And then I understood. "The war," I said. "Tell me about the war."

Aunt Memory shook her head.

"I am giving you a memory," she said. "There is an order to be followed, so you can remember it years from now."

I could see how this memory stuff could really get in the way. I wasn't entirely convinced, anyhow. But I kept my mouth shut.

"People lived in Crythe for centuries, keeping the old traditions alive," she said. "We were in mountains, off the main trade routes, so there was little threat from the outside world. When we heard of some modernization beyond our village, we'd send a young man out to learn all about it and report back to the village elders. If it sounded useful, we'd adopt it and bring it into our homes. Indoor plumbing. Electricity. Telephones. But if it sounded like too much of a waste of memory, we'd leave it alone, just as the world left us alone. An ideal setup. Until 1986. Our Year of Horror."

"The war started then?" I asked. I was doing the math in my head. I wasn't even born yet in 1986. If the war started then and was still going on—

"No," Aunt Memory said impatiently. I don't think she expected me to keep interrupting with questions. "What befell us then was a world tragedy, one you've undoubtedly learned about."

I racked my brain. *Nineteen eighty-six, nineteen eighty-six.* It didn't ring any bells.

"I'm sorry," I said. "They teach us 1492 and 1776, but beyond that, my history teachers haven't really bothered much with dates."

Aunt Memory looked as horrified as if I'd confessed that I couldn't read.

"Chernobyl," she said.

Sixteen

"HUH?" I SAID. THE WORD WASN'T EVEN OUT OF MY mouth before I realized I should have at least pretended to be thinking hard, remembering. I could have used one of those classic ignorant-student lines like, *Oh, yes, of course. Chernobyl. I'm sure you know a lot more than I do—why don't you tell me all about it?*

Aunt Memory now looked as though she wondered whether I even had a brain.

"Chernobyl," she repeated, through gritted teeth. "The nuclear meltdown at the power plant in the former Soviet Union? Crythe was right in the pathway of the worst of the radiation." She waited, as if she wasn't sure I would understand all those words.

"Yes?" I said.

Aunt Memory cupped her hands around her mug of tea, very precisely.

"It wasn't ever publicized, but the United States and the Soviet Union had an unprecedented moment of cooperation. They were bitter enemies then, you know. But they evacuated our entire village. They brought us here. And we recreated our village exactly as it was. We chose not to even talk about our old homeland. *This* is Crythe now. The only Crythe. Understand?"

I nodded, because that was what she seemed to expect. But my mind was churning with questions. Why hadn't the Crythians just moved somewhere closer to their original homes—at least on the same continent? What did this have to do with me? I decided to cover my confusion by taking a drink of my tea, but I'd forgotten it too long. It was cold and unappealing.

"But the move brought . . . disagreements to our peaceful community. The Americans wanted to study us, to make sure no one had been affected by the radiation. Some thought that was necessary. Others worried that they'd find out more than they should know and treat us as . . . oddities." Aunt Memory seemed to be choosing her words very carefully. She was looking straight into my eyes in a way that reminded me of being hypnotized. "Some saw all the technology the Americans had and wanted to use it to enhance our memories even more. Others worried that we would lose our old ways. Some . . . just wanted to fight."

"What did my parents want?" I asked in a small voice. "And Sophia?"

I saw a flicker of something—was it anger?—in Aunt Memory's eyes. But her expression stayed carefully bland. Maybe I'd imagined the anger.

"Well, of course you'd want to know that," she said in a soothing tone. "Of course." She glanced around the kitchen. "More tea first?"

I shook my head. Surely she could see I hadn't even drunk the tea I had.

"All right, then." She got up and bustled about, preparing herself some more tea. She didn't speak again until she was sitting down, a fresh mug in front of her. "Your father volunteered to investigate computers for Crythe. And he took to them immediately. His mind worked that way. But ultimately he feared that they would . . . interfere with our lives. Our memories. He recommended that they be prohibited from Crythe forever. And that was why he was killed."

I gasped.

"And my real mother?" I asked.

"She was executed at the same time as he," Aunt Memory said. "For the same reason."

Aunt Memory was watching my reaction very carefully, and that was why I had to be very careful not to react. I didn't let myself think about what any of this meant.

"And my—I mean, Sophia?" I whispered.

Aunt Memory was looking at the clock above the old-fashioned stove.

"It is late," she said. "Past midnight. We've talked enough for now. Tomorrow you'll read your statement to the entire village. Then you can ask all the questions you want."

She showed me to a room on the second floor. Its wallpaper had tiny pink rosebuds. Toys lined the walls: a rocking horse, a kite, a wooden train. I stopped at the threshold.

"This room—," I murmured.

"You recognize it? Very good. This was your nursery, all those years ago. It's been kept the same. But now you'll be sleeping in your nurse's old bed, not the crib, of course. The bathroom is through that door. Good night."

Dazed, I walked around the room, sliding my fingers along the curve of the rocking chair, the post of the bed. I had the eeriest feeling. Did I really remember this room? Or did I just believe I did because of what Aunt Memory said? I couldn't re-create in my mind what I'd been thinking when it first seemed familiar.

More than a little spooked, I shut the door behind me.

I found my suitcase beside my bed and shivered opening it. Aunt Memory had given me so much to think about that I'd forgotten about the suitcase; now I could finally find out why it was so heavy.

But it felt light now. And when I unzipped it, it contained only my jeans and sweatshirts, underwear and toothbrush, all jumbled together. I tried to refold the clothes more neatly, but my hands were shaking. I dropped my favorite Ohio State sweatshirt. When I bent down to pick it up, I heard a voice.

"Kira, whatever you do, don't scream," it whispered from under the bed. "You're alone now, aren't you?"

I swallowed the scream that had been forming in my throat. It came out as a yelp. I whipped back the dust ruffle of the bed.

And there, with lint in her hair, more than a thousand miles from home, was my best friend.

Seventeen

"LYNNE?" I SAID IN DISBELIEF. AFTER EVERYTHING
else that had happened that evening, I wasn't sure I
could trust even what I saw with my own eyes. I
wouldn't have been surprised if everything that
had happened since I got home from school today
was a hallucination. "What— How—?"

Lynne raised her head, clunking it on the
frame of the bed. I giggled nervously but with
some relief. Things like that don't happen in hal-
lucinations. Do they?

"Shh," she said, putting a finger to her lips.

"Don't you want to come out from there?" I
asked. She had dust bunnies on her jeans. Some of
her hair was caught in the bedsprings, just inches
above her head.

"Believe me, I'd rather be just about anywhere
else but lying on this hard floor," she whispered
back. "But I don't think it's safe. Keep your voice

down. And pretend I'm not here if anyone comes in. Act normal."

Oh, yeah, I'd look very normal if anyone came in. I always lie on the floor talking to beds.

"Are you out of your mind?" I asked Lynne.

"Are you?" Lynne retorted. "Letting a stranger into your house, agreeing to get in a car with a total stranger—"

"I did change my mind about that," I defended myself. "But how did you know? How did you get here?"

Lynne sighed.

"I was walking over to your house from the library. You'd sounded so weird on the phone that I told my dad to go on home, that I'd just spend the night at your house when I got done at the library. Then I saw this strange woman walking up your stairs. I didn't intend to eavesdrop, but you did have your windows open. . . ."

I thought about what Lynne had overheard.

"And then it looked like you were actually going to go someplace with that wacko," she continued. "I hid in the bushes. I wanted to see the license plate. I had my cell phone with me; I was going to dial 911 as soon as you drove away. But it was too dark to see the plate. The trunk was open—I didn't stop to think. I climbed in. I hid in your suitcase—believe me, that thing's not easy to zip from the inside. But I did it. I thought that was the only way I could help you. I thought I could call 911 from the car, they could track my signal—"

"So did you call?" I asked eagerly. I was suddenly overwhelmed with gratitude at having a friend like Lynne. So ingenious, so loyal, so reliable. After all the confusing things Aunt Memory had told me, it would be wonderful to see police officers, deputy sheriffs—anyone with authority—burst into the room, take charge, straighten everything out.

"Um . . ." Lynne wouldn't look me in the eye. "My battery was dead. I forgot to turn the phone off after using it to call the bank. I'm really sorry."

My heart sank.

"For a genius, you're a real idiot, you know that?" I hissed. Then I felt guilty. "But I do appreciate—you know. You didn't have to be in this mess. I do. Hey, maybe you can figure everything out."

"What *is* going on?" Lynne demanded.

Lying on the floor, my cheek pressed against a braided rug, I told Lynne everything I could remember of Aunt Memory's explanation. I wished I had Crythian abilities, Lynne kept asking questions I couldn't answer.

"Did this Aunt Memory say the original Crythe was part of the old Soviet Union?"

"I think so." I bit my lip, trying to remember. "I

mean, she said they were right in the path of the radiation from Chernobyl, and that was in Russia, right?"

"Ukraine," Lynne muttered. "And they worried about the radiation blowing across all of Europe, so Crythe could have been lots of different places."

"Why does it matter?" I asked. My face was becoming one with the braided rug. My teeth had that fuzzy feeling that meant they really needed to be brushed. I was more tired than I'd ever been, even after staying up all night at a sleepover. I just wanted to go to bed and pray that when I woke up, I'd be in my own bed back home and everything since my hypnosis would just be a weird dream.

"Every detail is important," Lynne said. "Because Aunt Memory has to be lying, and we've got to figure out if any of her wild tale is true."

I just looked at Lynne. She's the most confident person I know, and usually I admired that. But no one in her right mind would stay confident lying on the floor under a bed, with nothing but a dead cell phone and unknown danger all around.

"Yeah?" I said. "Just because her story's weird doesn't mean it isn't true."

Lynne shook her head.

"Come on, Kira. How could someone remember *everything* that ever happened to her? Every time she tied her shoes. Every time she brushed her teeth. Every time she washed her hands. It's so—so boring. Tedious. You can't remember all that."

"*You* probably could," I teased.

"No, I couldn't," Lynne said. "And I wouldn't want to."

Lynne had an odd look on her face.

"You're jealous," I said. "You wish you were Crythian."

"I do not!" Lynne insisted.

Somebody knocked at the door. I froze.

"Is okay in?" a man's heavily accented voice called out.

I dropped the dust ruffle, hiding Lynne. Then I scrambled to my feet. I walked to the door and yanked on the knob.

Two men in those gray-jacketed uniforms were in the hall. They stood erect, on either side of my door. They had not just been walking past. They were guards, sentries.

"I'm fine," I said. "I was just, uh, talking to myself." Both men looked puzzled. "It, uh, helps me think," I explained. "I think out loud." I decided babbling like that sounded suspicious. I shut up.

Both men gave me the same measuring look Aunt Memory had used on me. I didn't like being examined that closely. I had the feeling they were memorizing every strand of hair that I had out of place. I probably had a faint imprint of the braided rug on the side of my face; they were probably even now deducing that I'd been talking to someone under my bed.

"So, um, I'm fine. You can go on now. I'm sure you two are tired too," I said, trying to hide my desperation.

Neither man moved.

"We here," the older of the two said. "We keep you safe."

"Um, thanks," I said, defeated. "That's very nice of you, I'm sure. Um, good night."

I shut the door, but I did not go back to Lynne. I went into the bathroom, washed my face, brushed my teeth, changed into my usual night-wear, sweats and a T-shirt. I was trying so hard to make normal, all-by-myself noises that I'm sure I was suspiciously loud.

When I finally went back to the bed, Lynne had slipped a piece of paper just far enough out for me to see. I cautiously bent down and picked it up.

Who or what are they protecting you from?
Or are they imprisoning you?
Why won't Aunt Memory tell you "every-thing else" before you make your statement tomorrow?

"I don't know," I whispered. I didn't want to think about any of those questions.

Lynne shoved another scrap of paper out at me: *Does your door lock?* it said.

I bent over, lifted the dust ruffle, and shook my head at Lynne. No. Of course it didn't lock. She sighed silently, grimacing.

"Do you want to talk some more?" I asked in my softest voice.

Lynne shook her head. *Go to sleep*, she mouthed.

I climbed into the bed, willing it to be hard— which was what I deserved, given where Lynne was going to be sleeping. But the bed was soft and welcoming, a haven. Had my nurse ever put me down for naps on this bed, years and years ago? Had my real mother ever sat on this bed, watching me play? Had I belonged here all along?

Eighteen

IN THE MORNING THE COMFORTER WAS MISSING FROM my bed. I found it and Lynne tangled together in the bathtub. I shut the bathroom door and turned the water on full-blast in the sink to cover the noise of us talking.

"Lynne?" I said. "Wake up. There might be maids or, I don't know, cleaning ladies coming through."

Lynne didn't move. "Go 'way," she groaned, her eyes still shut.

"Lynne!" I pleaded.

Lynne opened one eye halfway.

"Do you know how hard that floor was?" she asked.

"You're not on the floor anymore," I said.

Lynne grimaced. "Yeah, I decided a little risk was better than a sleepless night, so I moved in here, as the next safest place to hide. But do you know how hard this tub is, too?"

"Sorry," I muttered. The water roared in the sink behind me.

Lynne opened her other eye.

"They'll know we're missing today," she said. "When we don't show up for school. They'll call home, and my parents will go crazy with worry."

Her parents would. I wondered, if the situation were reversed, and it was Mom back home in Willistown and me chasing after Lynne, if Mom would even notice me gone.

"But that's good," I argued. "Maybe they can track us down, save us, and Mom, too."

"How in the world would they track us here?" Lynne asked.

"Oh," I said. I hadn't gotten enough sleep. I couldn't think straight. The sight of all that running water in the sink suddenly made me want to cry. "What are we going to do?" I appealed to Lynne.

"You're going to ask to have breakfast sent up to your room, so we can share, instead of me trying to survive on the one measly stick of gum I have in my backpack," Lynne said. "And then I'm going to sneak out and find the nearest pay phone."

I was impressed. Just three minutes awake from a miserable night's sleep and Lynne already had her day planned. She'd have us rescued in no time.

"Now, turn that water off," Lynne said. "They're going to think you're drowning yourself."

I showered and was in the middle of getting dressed when someone knocked on the door. I finished putting on my T-shirt and waited until Lynne slipped back under the bed before I called out, "Yes?"

Aunt Memory thrust open the door. She had a huge swath of fabric draped over her arm— orange and yellow and green, brilliant colors, practically shining in the sunlight streaming in through my window.

"Your ceremonial dress," she announced. "For this morning's speech."

She shifted her grasp to the top of the piled fabric and lifted it up, and I saw that it was really a dress. It wasn't constructed like any I'd ever seen before. I tried to think of words to describe it—"kimono"? "sari"? "dirndl"?—and rejected them all. This dress had layers of skirts flowing out from the waist and just as many layers of sleeves flowing from the bodice.

"You said—," I started. "You said my jeans and sweatshirts were fine."

"Well, for the trip, certainly. But this is an important speech you'll be making. You'll want to look your best. And people will expect . . . this."

She gave the dress a little shake and it shimmied before my eyes.

"Oh," I said. I swallowed hard. "So now it's a speech I'm making? Before it was just an appeal. A statement."

"It's all the same," Aunt Memory assured me. "Appeal, statement, speech—why does it matter what we call it?"

"Okay, okay. Whatever," I said. My stomach chose that moment to growl, and I remembered Lynne's idea. "Um, I'm kind of nervous about that speech. Do you suppose I could just have some breakfast sent up to my room beforehand?"

"Of course!" Aunt Memory said. "What a good idea. I'll eat here with you."

Oops. That hadn't been what I had in mind.

But Aunt Memory was already stepping over to the door and conferring with one of the guards.

"Sausage and eggs sound good?" Aunt Memory asked over her shoulder.

I was calculating how I could slip something under the bed. Sausage and eggs wouldn't work.

"Um, and fruit," I said quickly. "Apples and oranges. Lots of them. And maybe some toast."

Ten awkward minutes later Aunt Memory

and I were sitting at a table brought in just for us, over huge platters of everything we'd asked for. I kept wishing Aunt Memory would take her eyes off me for just a second, so I could slip an apple and an orange into my pocket for Lynne. Then when I took off my sweatshirt, I could slide it under the bed. . . . My mind was going a million miles a minute.

Aunt Memory kept watching me. Silently.

"Um, this is very good," I said, though I was too nervous to actually taste anything.

"Taste is very closely linked to memory," Aunt Memory said. "In fact, we use that in some of our very first memory sessions, when we are training children. What do you remember when you are tasting that?" She pointed to the piece of sausage on the fork I was bringing to my mouth.

I bit and chewed and swallowed.

"Saturday mornings at my friend Lynne's house," I said. "The seasoning is different, but that's the only place I ever eat sausage."

For some reason, tears stung in my eyes.

"See how powerful memory is?" Aunt Memory murmured.

Angrily, I rubbed the tears away. I'd been thinking about Lynne under the bed now, in danger now, not safely at her house like all those Saturdays in the past.

"Why does memory matter so much in Crythe?" I asked. "What's so wrong about forgetting something every now and then?"

Aunt Memory looked aghast.

"Oh, my dear," she said. "How can you even ask that? But, of course, you were not raised properly. . . . We have a saying in Crythe: *Mogha laha dahr sa.* I believe it would translate as, 'Why live if you don't remember?' No, no—that's too trite. It's more like, 'Life is best lived many times.' If you remember, you can experience every moment of your life many times. So it's like having many lives."

"What about bad memories?" I challenged. "What if you only want to experience something once?"

Finally, finally, Aunt Memory glanced away from me. But it wasn't long enough. I didn't even have time to reach for an apple before her gaze was back on my face.

"Even that which is not enjoyable must be relived," she said sternly. "You will still learn from it."

I squirmed. I wished Lynne were out with me, asking the questions. I didn't care about all this memory stuff. There was too much else I needed to understand.

"Could you—I mean, would you explain

more, like what you were telling me last night?" I asked. "I still don't know how I can get the kidnappers to release Mom."

"Oh, but that's all taken care of. I have your speech right here," Aunt Memory said, patting her pocket. "I'll give it to you after breakfast."

This bothered me, that Aunt Memory expected me to say whatever she told me to say. Like a puppet. I didn't know how to complain, though. Another problem occurred to me too.

"Will there be a translator?" I asked.

"Oh, no. All Crythians have learned English."

I thought of the pilot I'd assumed could not understand me. Maybe I should have appealed to him. Or asked him questions. Maybe it would have done some good.

But I was so ignorant, I didn't even know the questions to ask. Unlike Lynne, I had no faith in being able to tell when people were lying. I was totally the wrong person to be here in this strange place, trying to decipher this strange woman's cryptic comments.

I was beginning to feel panicky. I pushed my plate of food away.

"Full already?" Aunt Memory said. Of course she'd noticed how little I'd eaten.

"I'm getting nervous about the speech," I said, which was true, if not the entire truth. "But I might be hungry later. Could I keep this bowl of fruit in my room?"

Inspired, I thought. Lynne should be proud.

I'd already picked up the bowl of fruit and was carrying it over to the nightstand beside the bed before Aunt Memory answered.

"Oh, you won't be spending much time in your room today," she said. "I assure you, you can eat anytime you want. Leaving food in your room is so—so messy."

Strategically, I tripped on the rug and dropped the bowl. At least two apples and an orange rolled under the bed. I only pretended to retrieve them.

I hoped Lynne appreciated what I'd gone through to get her breakfast.

Nineteen

AUNT MEMORY DIDN'T LEAVE MY ROOM EVEN TO LET
me change into the ceremonial dress. She slipped
it over my head for me and began murmuring,
"And don't you look lovely," even before it had
completely settled on my shoulders. The dress fit
okay, but I didn't feel right with it on. I felt like a
woman from the past. This dress was not nearly as
confining as, say, a hoopskirt and corsets, but
every step set off a wave of ripples in all the layers
of fabric. It would have been impossible to walk
quickly in this dress.

"That's it! Time to go!" Aunt Memory said as I
took my first few experimental steps around the
room.

"But—my speech—," I protested. "I haven't
even looked at it."

"Oh, you can read it on the spot," Aunt
Memory said. "Here it is. Come on!"

She thrust pages into my hand and hurried me out the door. I tried to look at the speech, but the carpet was uneven and I almost tripped. The guards or sentries or whatever they were saluted as I went past.

"Come, come," Aunt Memory urged me on. "The people are waiting."

And then we burst out the front door, back to the street we'd driven on the night before. But now the street was completely blocked by a throng of people. The women did indeed wear kerchiefs and full peasant skirts. The men were in rough woven pants and billowy shirts. I saw no children. I stood hesitantly in the doorway, blinking in the sunlight. Aunt Memory stepped to the side, exposing me to the entire crowd. Immediately a hush fell over them. They stared at me. And then they began cheering.

"The child has returned!" someone yelled.

"Kira Landanova is back," someone else hollered. And then the whole crowd began chanting along: "She is back! Kira Landanova is back!"

I felt my cheeks turning red, then redder still. The people before me kept chanting.

Who was I, to be greeted like this? Bewildered and overwhelmed, I looked down at the papers in my hand, hoping they'd give some clue.

Greetings. I am Kira Landanova, daughter of Alexei

and Victoriana, the first page began. I stopped on my mother's name. Victoriana . . . No wonder I'd thought the term "Victorian houses" sounded familiar all those years ago. My real mother. The crowd still cheered, but somehow I could barely hear them. My mind was in a whirl. Alexei and Victoriana. They were the ones I belonged to. Not Mom. But my mind was a traitor: Suddenly all I could think about was how Mom had taken care of me for the last thirteen years. She'd cleaned up my vomit when I'd gotten sick. She'd cut up my meat for me when I was too little to handle knives. She'd held my hand crossing streets on my first day of school. . . .

I remembered that I was here to rescue Mom, not to be cheered and praised. I glanced down at the rest of the speech. Phrases jumped out at me: *We must return to our old traditions . . . My parents would have wanted you to obey your leaders . . . What my parents stood for was Crythe at its finest* . . . It was a political speech. How was this supposed to help Mom?

Aunt Memory nudged me with her elbow.

"You must begin," she said, but I could barely hear her over the crowd and the ringing in my ears.

"Greetings," I began. I was certain it was hopeless trying to make myself heard. But by the time I got to "Kira Landanova," the entire crowd was silent, waiting for my next word. It was eerie, the attention they all gave me. Every eye bored straight into mine. Even if I hadn't known a thing about Crythe, I still would have felt like every syllable I uttered was being instantly memorized and treasured. Not even a bird sang to interrupt me.

I stumbled over the next words, " . . . daughter of Alexei and—and Victoriana—"

And then I stopped. The next sentence on Aunt Memory's paper said, *In the name of my parents, I ask you to turn your back on the rash decisions of the past thirteen years.* But I didn't know what those decisions were. I didn't know what my parents would have wanted me to say. I didn't even know what Mom would want me to say. All I had to go on was Aunt Memory's explanations.

I thought about what Lynne had said the night before, about figuring out if anything Aunt Memory said was true. I wished I had Lynne here with me now, to tell me what to do. I'd say just about anything to help Mom. But the way the people were watching me, the way Aunt Memory was watching me—none of this was about Mom.

It had been a long time now since I'd said my last word. If a speaker was silent this long at a school assembly, back home in Willistown, everyone would be whispering now, muttering, *What an idiot!* and *Who wanted to hear her, anyway?* But this crowd in Crythe stayed quiet, kept waiting. A

slight breeze blew down the street, ruffling kerchiefs, lifting locks of hair. But the people kept
still, like statues who expected me to bring them
back to life.

I dropped Aunt Memory's speech.

"I—I am Kira Landon," I repeated, only barely
conscious that I'd truncated the name Aunt
Memory had assigned me and turned it back into
the name I'd used for as long as I could remember. "I'm told that my parents were Alexei and
Victoriana. I want to believe that, because I am
eager to find out about my past. I had not even
heard of Crythe until yesterday. I don't know
your customs or your history or—or your strug-
gles right now. All I know is that the woman who
raised me disappeared yesterday. I believe she was
kidnapped and brought here. And, whoever took
her, please set her free. She is very—I mean . . . I
love her. I miss her."

I had nothing else to say. I stepped back. The
pages of Aunt Memory's speech lay scattered at
my feet. They rustled in the breeze.

I dared to turn toward Aunt Memory. She
looked as though I'd slapped her. Fury shone in
her eyes. I peered back out at the crowd, expecting—I don't know. Questions, maybe. But they
still weren't speaking or moving. Then I saw that
they were—they were moving only their eyes and,

ever so slightly, their heads. They were exchanging furtive, fearful glances.

I could not understand these people. I didn't know what they wanted from me.

Aunt Memory stepped in front of me. With one hand, she reached back and clutched my right wrist, her fingers tight as a vise. I would have felt less trapped in handcuffs.

"All honor to Kira Landanova, daughter of Alexei and Victoriana!" she proclaimed, raising her fist. The crowd obediently repeated her words. Then Aunt Memory let out a stream of Crythian words. She did not sound angry. She sounded proud, excited, triumphant. Maybe she was giving the speech she'd written for me. But every time her voice crescendoed, she squeezed my wrist tighter.

Had I made a mistake, angering Aunt Memory? Would it have mattered if I'd spoken the words she'd wanted to put in my mouth? Had I endangered Mom?

Suddenly, without warning, Aunt Memory finished her speech. She pulled me up beside her and raised my arm for me. I'm sure that, from the audience, it looked like I was willingly joining in the victorious gesture. We stood there for a long time, being admired. Maybe I could have broken away, run out into the crowd, assured them that, whatever Aunt Memory had said, she wasn't speaking for me. But I was too dazed. And I didn't expect what came next.

Just when my arm was beginning to ache from being held in the air for so long, Aunt Memory brought both of our arms down. Without relaxing her iron grip on my wrist, she bowed deeply, then stepped backward. She yanked me back into the castle with her. Instantly a guard swung the door shut behind me.

"What was that all about?" Aunt Memory hissed angrily at me.

"I just—I just said what I knew was right. The way they were looking at me—like they trusted what I said—I couldn't say anything I wasn't sure of. And Crythian politics—I don't know anything about that. All I have to go on is what you told me." I realized how that must have sounded. "No offense," I added lamely.

Aunt Memory looked like she'd taken plenty of offense.

"You might have just killed Sophia," she said.

I went numb. Aunt Memory shoved me up the stairs and practically hurled me into my room. She stalked out, slamming the door behind her.

Sobbing, I crumbled to the floor in a heap of green and orange and yellow skirts.

Twenty

I DIDN'T THINK FOR A LONG TIME. IT WAS EASIER JUST to sob and sob and sob. But finally, I raised my head and whispered, "Lynne?"

No answer.

Shakily, I got to my feet and stumbled over to the bed. I peeked underneath. Two apple cores lay atop a neat pile of orange rinds. But there was no other evidence that Lynne had ever been here.

I looked in the bathtub, too, just in case, but it was empty.

I should have been delighted that she got out, that she was going for help right now. But I felt bereft. I wanted her there to tell me I'd done the right thing. To tell me I shouldn't feel like I'd just killed the person who mattered most to me in all the world.

Funny, how I was thinking of Mom differently now.

Maybe they'd caught Lynne, too, when she was sneaking out, and she wasn't getting help right now, she was being tortured. Maybe even killed. And that would also be my fault.

I sank onto the floor of the bathroom and cried some more. I was so scared.

"This is not my life," I whimpered. "This is not where I belong. This is not *me*."

If I hadn't had tears streaming down my face, I would have bounced up right then and gone in search of Aunt Memory. I wanted to tell her she had the wrong person. I was Kira Landon, from dinky old Willistown. My mother was a librarian, for Pete's sake. The biggest problem in my life was supposed to be that it was dull.

Lynne would have said I was seriously in denial.

But Lynne had also said that Aunt Memory lied.

I pulled a towel down from the rack beside me and wiped my eyes on it. I stood up and peered at my tear-splotched face in the mirror.

"Aunt Memory is not going to know what hit her," I muttered to my reflected image. "I'm going to find out the truth."

Five minutes later I was out of the confining ceremonial dress and back into my jeans and sweatshirt. That alone made me feel more like myself. I washed my face and combed my hair back into a neat ponytail. I pulled my tennis shoes back on and tied the laces with unusually precise loops. I felt like a soldier preparing for battle.

I opened the door. Once again, there were two men in uniforms standing there. They sprang to attention. I stepped out over the threshold.

"Oh, no, miss," one said.

"*Stanahla*," the other said. "Honorable young lady—"

I drew back. I remembered Lynne's questions the night before about the guards: *Who or what are they protecting you from? Or are they imprisoning you?* Well, I was about to find out. I forced myself to step forward again. The guards flailed their arms and rushed toward me.

"Miss, miss, no," the first one said. "Not safe."

"What's not safe?" I challenged.

"You come—coming—out," the guard said. He put his arm out, firm against my waist, holding me back.

"I need to talk to my Aunt Memory," I said, trying to sound calm, reasonable, unfazed. My voice shook. I sounded terrified.

The guard tilted his head to the side, studying me. I studied him back. He was older than the other guard. Hints of gray shone through his blue-black hair and streaked his beard.

Blue-black hair. I'd never met anyone with hair like mine before, but his was. My heart thumped. The hair proved something; this guard and I were connected somehow. But was he my bodyguard or my jailer? That was the more important question.

"You stay," the guard finally said. "There." He pointed, as if he didn't trust me to understand his English. "I go. Get her."

I retreated, not willing to test them. I saw no evidence that either of them carried a gun, but there were two of them and one of me. If I tried to make a run for it, I probably wouldn't even make it to the stairs.

"Okay," I said. "Could you please hurry?"

The older guard started walking down the hall, glancing back cautiously every few paces. I did not shut the door. I looked at the other guard.

"You are Crythian, right?" I asked.

He nodded.

"Do you understand when I speak in English?" I asked.

"Understand, yes," he said. "Make words me, bad."

It took me a while to interpret that. His apologetic expression helped.

"You mean, you can understand English better than you can speak it?"

He nodded again. This was not very helpful.

"I don't remember any Crythian," I said.

He shrugged. A red blush crept up his cheeks, a strange sight. He was embarrassed for me. Good grief. He was acting like he'd seen me naked or something.

"Could you teach me some Crythian words?" I asked.

Now he shifted on his feet and looked around, as if longing for the other guard to come back.

"It is easy to learn," he said. "It is hard to forget."

Why would I bother learning it if I wanted to forget?

I didn't know what to say after that, and the guard didn't seem to either. He stared straight ahead, his eyes fixed on a point on the opposite wall. If Aunt Memory was right, he was going to remember that little patch of rose wallpaper the rest of his life.

Ridiculous.

I heard footsteps on the stairs then. The older guard was coming back, with Aunt Memory walking regally behind him.

When they reached my doorway, the guard humbly stepped back, letting her past. She looked at me coldly.

"Well?" she said.

"I have questions," I said. "I need to know—everything. You told me that after the speech you would explain—" I stopped. It was hard to keep talking to someone whose face was so set.

Aunt Memory looked from one guard to the other. She frowned warningly at them, then stepped into my room and shut the door behind us. I went to sit at the small round table where we'd had breakfast, but she kept standing. After a moment I stood back up too.

"Crythians do not ask questions," she said. "It is not proper. You are a disgrace to Crythe."

"How was I to know?" I begged. "I wasn't raised in Crythe. It's natural for me to wonder."

"I told you what you needed to know last night," she said. "I tolerated your questions then, because of your ignorance. But after this morning—" She gave me a bitter grin. "Why should I answer your questions when you do not believe me?"

"I didn't say that!" I protested.

"'All I have to go on is what you told me,'" she said, exactly mimicking the words I'd spoken barely an hour earlier.

"I didn't—that's not what I meant," I said lamely. "It's just . . . you didn't tell me enough. I need to know all about Crythe and the people here, so I can think about it, figure out my own viewpoint, make my own decisions."

I could tell making your own decisions was about as popular in Crythe as asking questions. Aunt Memory had stiffened even more, if that was possible.

"Tell me about Mom. Sophia," I said quickly. "Who was she in Crythe? Did she know my parents? How did she kidnap me? Why?"

"Give the speech first," Aunt Memory said. "The proper speech I prepared for you."

"Why is it so important that I say those exact words?" I asked.

Aunt Memory just looked at me. Waiting.

I am not a resolute person. I'm not the type to stand up for myself. I've mostly glided through life doing what people expect me to do. Why had I picked today to develop backbone?

Maybe it was because of that patronizing way Aunt Memory kept looking at me. I didn't want to be the kind of person who deserved that look.

"No," I said. "I can't give that speech until I understand what it means. And if it means something I don't agree with . . . well, then, I'm sorry."

"Sophia's life is not worth anything to you?"

"No, I didn't say that," I wailed. "But the way you're setting this up—it isn't fair. It's blackmail."

"I see," Aunt Memory said quietly. "Come with me, then."

I followed her out of the room, past the

guards, down the hall. I didn't know where we were going, and I didn't ask. I felt like I'd won our little war of words, though. I almost expected to be led into a library, lined with shelves of books titled *Secrets of Crythe*. And soon I would know all those secrets.

Aunt Memory began climbing down the stairs, with me on her heels. The carpet was soft and plush and luxurious; either the Crythians had had a lot of money when they'd left their old village, or they'd made a lot once they came to California. But what was there to make money at, out here in the middle of nowhere?

We were on the first floor now. Aunt Memory didn't speak. She led me back to the kitchen and to a strange door. I thought perhaps it led to the backyard, but stairs gaped up at us as soon as she opened the door. Aunt Memory began climbing down, into a basement. She pulled the chain hanging from a single lightbulb overhead. The basement was huge but bare, totally empty, just cinder-block walls and a concrete floor. I looked around, bewildered, wondering why she'd brought me here. There wasn't a single *Secrets of Crythe* book in sight.

Aunt Memory motioned me over to a door on the far wall.

"What—," I started to ask, but she put her finger to her lips.

She unlocked the door with a key she drew out from her skirt pocket. It was dark beyond the door, but Aunt Memory gave me a little shove forward. I stumbled into the darkness. Aunt Memory switched on the light.

And there, lying on the floor, was Mom.

Twenty-One

SHE SEEMED TO BE SLEEPING, HER HEAD ON A PILLOW on the floor, her gray hair loose and flowing over her shoulders like a blanket.

"You found her!" I raved. "You got her back from the kidnappers! How?" I didn't wait for an answer. "Mom! Mom! Are you okay? Wake up! I'm here! Kira! You're safe now!"

I could have done a dance, right there on the concrete, I was so overjoyed. Mom and I were together again, we could go back to Willistown now, never have to worry about crazy Crythe again. I didn't care anymore about the past or my real parents or my—what had Aunt Memory called it?—my heritage. It was all too confusing, and it didn't seem to matter much. Not to me, anyway.

Mom's eyelids fluttered, and the sight sent a jolt of relief through my body. Belatedly, I realized:

Lying like that, she could have been dead. But she wasn't; she was opening her eyes now, staring up at me. Why was she lying on the floor in this little room? I didn't want to think about it. I bent over and grabbed her hand—never mind that neither of us was big on all that touchy-feely stuff. I grabbed her hand and practically clutched it. Mom's eyes focused on my face.

"Oh no," she said. "You."

The words chilled me. I didn't want to understand them.

"Now, that's a fine greeting," I chided her jokingly. "I come all this way to rescue you, and that's the thanks I get?"

Mom kept staring at me.

"Come on," I said. "Let's get you out of here." I put my arm under her neck and started to lift her up. I don't know what I had in mind—maybe one of those hero moments, a firefighter carrying an unconscious victim out of a burning building, a police officer pulling an injured child from a car wreck. I just knew: Aunt Memory and I were going to save Mom.

That's when I heard the click of the door latch behind me. And then . . . a key in the lock, turning. Locking us in.

"No!" I wailed.

I sprang back to the door, grabbed the handle,

turned with all my might. Or tried to. It didn't give. I pounded my fists on the door, screamed as loud as I could, "Aunt Memory! Aunt Memory! Let us out!"

I went hoarse, screaming. I don't know when I would have stopped, except that I felt Mom's hand on my head, stroking my hair.

"Oh, Kira," she said. "Oh, Kira."

I slumped against the door. Mom sat beside me, both of our backs against the unyielding metal.

"We're both prisoners now, aren't we?" I whispered.

Mom nodded. She wouldn't look at me. She just kept staring out at the tiny, bleak room.

"For the last two days," Mom said slowly, "the only thing that's kept me going is thinking about you, safe at Lynne's house. I've imagined you laughing and talking and eating those horrible Fritos and Chee-tos and M&M's, and drinking Coke, and thinking the biggest worry in the world is what grade you got on your geometry quiz. . . ."

"Mom," I protested, "even if I'd gone to Lynne's, I would have been worrying about you. I wouldn't have been able to laugh at all."

"Really?" Mom said, and she sounded surprised.

"Oh, Mom, of course," I said. "You're my

mother." The word echoed a little in the empty room. I froze. I'd forgotten what Aunt Memory had told me about my true parents. But how could I believe Aunt Memory now? Probably every word she'd spoken to me had been a lie. I wanted to ask Mom, just to be sure, but the words stuck in my throat.

Mom saw the confusion on my face.

"You know, don't you?" she asked quietly.

"Know what?" I said automatically. This was the voice I used to cover all my transgressions: "Curfew? What curfew?" "The last cookie? I didn't know there was only one left." "Parental permission slip? Was I supposed to have one of those?"

My voice of fake innocence sounded unnatural and entirely out of place in this empty room. This cell.

Mom was shaking her head.

"I think it is time for both of us to stop pretending," she said. "If I had told you the truth years ago . . ."

"What? I would have been prepared to be kidnapped?" I asked. "Hey, maybe you should have sent me to some sort of training, 'How to Be a Good Kidnap Victim.' I'm sure they offer it at the Willistown Y." I wanted Mom to laugh, but I'd forgotten again that Mom was my original kidnapper. Mom only looked grim.

"Mom, I still don't know much," I said. "Just what Aunt Memory told me. But she didn't like it when I asked questions, and I kept asking questions anyhow."

That's when Mom smiled.

"Good for you," she said.

"Yeah, but that's when she brought me here," I said. "And I wouldn't give the exact speech she wanted me to give, begging for your release."

Now alarm crept over Mom's face.

"What was in the speech?"

I told her everything I could remember. Mom just kept shaking her head.

"They're playing quite a game here," she murmured. "But you didn't say any of it?"

I shook my head emphatically. I told her what I'd said instead. She looked embarrassed.

"Well, um, thank you," she said, avoiding my eyes. "I didn't really know that you, um, loved me."

I got choked up and couldn't answer.

"Kira?" Mom said. "I shouldn't be, but I'm glad you're here with me."

And then I totally lost it and sobbed again, burying my face against Mom's shoulder.

Mom patted my back and murmured, "There, there, everything's okay," which was a lie, and both of us knew it. But it was still exactly what I wanted to hear. I probably sobbed longer than I needed to, just so Mom would keep comforting me.

Then I realized she'd stopped saying, "There, there," and was murmuring other words, practically to herself.

" . . . she had to have known that would hurt me most of all, pretending to be your Aunt Memory. To hear that name again, you screaming it, to *her*—"

"Mom?" I sat upright. "What are you talking about?"

"The lies you were told," Mom said. "Kira, it is true that I'm not your mother. But that doesn't mean that I didn't have the right to take you away from Crythe. You see . . . I'm your real Aunt Memory."

Twenty-Two

I STARED INTO MOM'S FACE. NO—MY TRUE AUNT Memory's face. No—Sophia's. I didn't know what to call her anymore, but this white, worried face in front of me was so familiar, I couldn't believe that names mattered.

"Explain," I said tersely.

Mom looked down at the concrete beneath us, and for a minute I was afraid that, after everything that had happened, she was still going to stonewall me. But then she looked straight at me and grimaced.

"I don't know where to start," she admitted.

"Aunt Memory—I mean, the woman who told me she was my Aunt Memory—she started with the Romans," I said. All these switched identities were too confusing. I had a mom who wasn't my mother, an Aunt Memory who wasn't my aunt, a mom who really was my Aunt Memory. . . . And to think, some of my friends back home thought their families were complicated just because they had a stepparent or two.

"The Romans? *She* would," Mom said bitterly. "Her real name is Rona Cummins, and she's not even Crythian. Or wasn't, to start out with."

I must have looked confused already because Mom laughed.

"Okay," she said. "The Romans. That's the legend, that Crythe was started by a noble, highly advanced group of Roman citizens fleeing the fall of the empire. But there's no proof, of course, because it's all oral history. Nothing was ever written down. I've suspected, since I left Crythe and became more, uh, cynical, that that's just a story someone chose to tell. If you don't know who your ancestors are, why not claim someone impressive, make yourself feel good?"

"But is it true or not?" I asked impatiently.

"Who knows?" Mom said. "The legend was passed down for generations, and so it's what Crythians remembered about themselves. So maybe it sort of became true, for Crythians."

I rubbed my forehead. Mom's explanation was going to be hard to follow.

"Crythe—the original Crythe—was high up in the mountains," she said. "It was achingly beautiful—oh, if you could see those peaks, covered in snow! Even a non-Crythian would not be able to forget Crythe. But it was not an easy place to live. For centuries, I think, people barely got by, barely managed to eke out an existence."

"Why didn't they just leave?" I asked.

"Oh, Kira, you are such an American," Mom said scornfully.

I felt scolded, put down.

"It's not my fault," I protested. "You're the one who made me an American. Right?"

Mom shook her head, but she looked amused.

"I deserve that," she said. "But you are so much what you are that I'm not sure you can understand Crythians. Americans believe that if you're not happy where you are, you pack up, you move, you go somewhere better. Or you go through a twelve-step program, you improve yourself. You leave the past behind. You think you've got a right to happiness, and you're going to make yourself happy even if it kills you."

"You're an American too," I pointed out.

Mom shrugged. "Maybe," she said. "I think I'm still more of a Crythian. Crythians believe in the past. They believe in memories. They do everything for memory, not for happiness."

"Yeah, yeah, I know," I said, not interested in all this philosophizing. What about my parents?

What about my kidnapping? But I was still curious about one other detail. "Aunt Mem—I mean, Rona—told me Crythians remember everything that ever happens to them. But that's not possible, is it?"

"Probably not," Mom admitted. "From the beginning, I think there were always details that Crythians forgot. The things that nobody cared about—the angle at which each blade of grass grew, the exact placement of each button in a button box—what did it matter if we remembered or forgot? But Crythians did have good memories. One Crythian left early in the twentieth century, and he created quite a stir, out in the Soviet Union. He worked as a journalist, and he could remember every interview without taking a single note. He did vaudeville-type shows, memorizing long strings of numbers or words and reciting them back perfectly. What he did was nothing a five-year-old Crythian couldn't do, but the rest of the world was amazed. He was written up in psychology texts. They called him 'S.'" The problem was, once he'd memorized all those meaningless numbers and words, he couldn't get them out of his mind. And so the psychologists taught him to forget."

Mom looked sad all of a sudden, and I couldn't think why.

"And then?" I prompted her. I was getting stiff

sitting on the cold floor. I shifted around, trying to sit sideways, but there was no way to get comfortable on the bare concrete.

"S was probably the reason Crythe came to the attention of the Soviet government. Or maybe not. It was years later, during the height of the Cold War . . . When they came to Crythe, they didn't explain. But since I left, I've done research. I read everything I could find about S. And I can just picture some Soviet leader coming across reports of his amazing feats, saying, 'Eureka! This has military applications!' Back then, that's all the Soviets and the Americans ever thought about, the military and having better weapons than the other side."

She was confusing me. "Since when is memory a weapon?" I asked.

Mom frowned, making me feel more ignorant than ever.

"Think about it," she said. "If you were a military leader, wouldn't you love to have pilots who needed to be told only once how to operate their planes? Or soldiers who could carry around complicated battle plans in their heads? Or electronics operators who never had to write down secret codes? Or—"

"Okay," I said. "I get it."

Mom shook her head, as if shaking off my

impatience. She pulled her hair back from her face, held it tight at the back of her head, released it.

"I was four years old when they came to Crythe," she finally said. She had a faraway look in her eye, as if there were a movie playing out on the opposite wall. All I saw was blank cinder blocks. "The Soviet officials came in jeeps—I'd never seen a jeep before," she said dreamily. "They began testing us, testing us all. And we were all too stupid or too naive or too proud to play dumb. We kids begged our Aunt Memories to train us harder than ever. We were like small-town starlets, dreaming of Hollywood."

I couldn't help dreading whatever she was going to say next.

"They picked twenty-five people, mostly kids. My sister Toria was the youngest. Just six."

"Toria? You mean Victoriana? My, my—" I couldn't say it, couldn't even get my lips to press together for the "m" in "mother."

Mom tore her gaze away from the invisible scene on the back wall and focused her eyes on me.

"Yes," she said. "Your mother was chosen. So was your father. Alexei was eight."

She gave me time to let that sink in. Or maybe she was giving herself time. I glanced down briefly, and when I looked back at her she was staring at the back wall again.

"I was so jealous," she said. "Mama said I was too young, but I was the typical little sister—convinced that anything Toria could do, I could do too.

"Then we found out they were taking the twenty-five away...."

I shivered. This was scarier than the ghost stories my friends and I told at sleepovers. Mom certainly looked haunted. She sat silent for a long time. I didn't prompt her to continue. Finally, she gave a little sigh and went on.

"When they came back, there were only six of them. Toria and Alexei would never tell us what they'd witnessed. They were strong, strong people. They'd lost a decade of their lives—most of their childhoods—to that horrible experiment. I think they were the only ones who returned sane. The other four were older. Men. They'd been in the Soviet Union's war in Afghanistan, and they still believed they were fighting it. You know the Vietnam veterans with post-traumatic stress syndrome? I think that was what they had, only worse, because they did not know how to forget anything. They could not stop reliving the past even for a moment. And Toria and Alexei were the only ones who could help them at all."

I tried to imagine my real mother, sixteen years old, a teenager, like me, helping war veterans instead of gulping down Diet Cokes and crying over stupid movies. She did not seem like a real person, this Toria.

"And then 1986 came, and it was not just the Soviet officials who came to warn us about the Chernobyl radiation," Mom continued. "Alexei figured that out, he knew what to say . . . he wanted to get us away."

"Aun—Rona said the Russians and the Americans cooperated, that they worked together," I protested.

Mom laughed.

"Now, that's an interesting lie," she said. "No—we were smuggled out, everyone in our entire village. Alexei said we knew military secrets we were ready to sell, we were each of us secret weapons. . . . I'm not even sure who he talked to, U.N. officials with American sympathies, maybe. But he was convincing. It's funny— a few years later the Americans would not have cared, the Cold War was over. But at that time the Americans still thought of the Soviet Union as the evil empire. They lived in fear that the Soviets would develop some all-powerful, secret weapon. So we were treated as highly valuable defectors. They helped us get land to build a new Crythe, an almost exact replica. I am not sure how Alexei strung them along. I can't imagine him betraying anyone. I think, perhaps, in the end, the Americans were not satisfied. Eventually, they stopped coming, the men in black cars. And then I think they forgot us. We had visas, we got citizenship, but we were just footnotes in the reports that nobody bothered to read anymore because the whole world had changed."

"I've never heard of anything like this in history class," I protested.

Mom gave me a scornful look.

"Oh, Kira, would you? Think for a minute about the thousands of lives that have never been written about. Think about the wars that have been fought that are never mentioned in your schools because they don't involve a single American or a single American interest—"

"There was a war in Crythe," I said. "The new Crythe."

Mom nodded.

"Yes. The officials didn't know about that, either." She was staring off into the distance again, talking as if in a trance. "We could have had peace. We could have just been those weirdos up in the mountains that nobody knew much about. But in America we broke down into factions. In our old land it was easy to live simply, forgetting nothing. But here—Leonid wanted a TV, Marta wanted the kind of kitchen she saw advertised in a magazine. . . . Then there were the extremists on the other side, those who wanted our village kept 'pure.' And both sides resented your parents."

"Why?" I asked. For the first time I felt possessive of them—Alexei and Toria—not quite Mom and Dad, but almost Mother and Father. My parents.

Mom sighed and finally looked back at me.

"Alexei and Toria were the only two who left the village on a regular basis, because they were going out to earn money for us. They were good with computers—their minds practically were computers. And back then a new idea with computers could make millions overnight, it seemed. You didn't need a college degree, you just needed to be smart and determined, and they were both. They were supporting the entire village, and people hated them for it."

I thought about how I'd felt toward Lynne over the years, the digs disguised as jokes: "Oh, you think you're so smart!" But Lynne was my friend. I didn't *hate* her.

"They were married by now," Mom continued. "They had you, but they hadn't forgotten the veterans of the Afghan war. And they weren't ignorant of the problems the extremists were causing in the village, expecting everyone to remember everything, punishing children for forgetting anything. . . ." Mom slowed down now, pacing her words as carefully as she'd steer a car alongside a dangerous cliff.

"They developed something with computers, to help some people remember, to help others forget. They were far ahead of their time. And what they did helped us all. But Crythians weren't satisfied. They wanted Alexei and Toria to—to sell their ideas. Some of the Crythians were greedy. And they found a buyer. Rona Cummins."

I jerked back. Everything so far had seemed like ancient history, from the Romans to my practically mythological parents. But that name— Rona Cummins—brought me back to the present. This wasn't just long-ago turmoil Mom was describing.

"Aunt Mem—I mean, this Rona—she said my parents disapproved of using computers in Crythe. She said that was why they were—" I couldn't finish.

"Rona Cummins would say anything to get what she wanted," Mom said disgustedly. "She was just manipulating you."

I felt more mixed up than ever.

"Did she want my parents to die?" I asked

weakly. It was less frightening than asking a more current question: Did she want me to die?

Mom shook her head. "She just wanted your parents' ideas. She didn't care how she got them. But she paid some of the more rabid Crythians to try to scare your parents into submitting. . . . It scared them into sending you away."

"With you," I said. "And that's what I remembered last Friday night, my real mother carrying me to you." I was sure of this suddenly. It was such a relief not to have any more doubts. "You didn't kidnap me."

"No," Mom said. "But you don't remember seeing me that night because you fell asleep in your mother's arms. She . . . she couldn't bear to say good-bye, so your father gave you to me. And then I carried you down the mountainside, and we found the car he'd hidden there. . . ." She seemed lost in memory. I realized suddenly that that was nothing new—every time over the past thirteen years that she'd seemed far away, distant, aloof, she'd really just been remembering.

"Why didn't my parents run away too?" I asked. "If they knew they were going to be killed—"

"They didn't know for sure," Mom said. "I think they must have had hope until the very end. I want to believe that." She grimaced, and I remembered that Toria had been Mom's sister. And Mom was like those Crythian war veterans, unable to leave the past behind. Mom was still grieving.

"They thought it was not honorable to abandon their people," Mom said. "They thought they could convince them. . . . Oh, Kira, there was already fighting when you and I escaped. I—I've read about wars, and they always seem so cut-and-dried in retrospect, so many troops lost, so much land taken, so many causes won. So neat and clean. But this war . . . this was people who'd known one another all their lives, shooting each other, point-blank. This was a man strangling his brother, bare-handed. This was a woman stabbing her neighbor in the back while she hung out her laundry." Mom spoke as if she were watching it all over again, as if everything were replaying before her eyes.

"Why?" I asked in horrified fascination.

"Like everything else in Crythe," Mom said, "because of memory."

For a second I almost felt Crythian. I knew I would never be able to forget the sight of Mom's face just then: the pale cheeks, the flowing tears, the anguish. She was weeping now. I'd never seen her weep before. I didn't want that image burned into my mind. I stood up stiffly and began pacing the floor, as if it might be possible to run away from everything Mom had told me. But the room was so small that I could take only five steps before I had to turn around. It was the same between the other walls—the room was practically a perfect square. I tapped on some of the cinder blocks, dug my fingernails into the mortar that held them together. But there were no weak spots.

"It's no use," Mom said, looking up at me through the tears. "The walls are solid. So is the floor. And the ceiling. I already tried. We can't escape."

I felt like the walls were closing in on me.

"What do they want from us?" I asked.

"Your parents' secrets," Mom said.

"But we don't have them," I protested. "Do we?"

Mom just kept looking at me. Strangely.

"Do you?" I asked.

Mom gave her head such a slight shake, it was barely perceptible. She kept watching me. She reminded me of those few teachers I'd had over the years who didn't keep talking when kids didn't understand, but just waited and waited.

I thought of drug smugglers who hid bags of cocaine in baby's diapers, I thought of Holocaust victims who swallowed valuable jewels to keep them from the Nazis. But Mom had spirited me out of Crythe thirteen years ago. Any diapers I'd worn then were long gone; anything I'd swallowed had passed through my system within days.

"Well, I'm sure I don't have any secrets that came from my parents," I said, trying to sound certain. "Can't we just tell them that?"

Mom's steady gaze was driving me crazy.

"Oh," she said slowly, "but that's where you're wrong. You see, you do have the secrets. You know them."

Twenty-Three

I FELT LIKE I'D BEEN ON ONE OF THOSE AMUSEMENT park rides that batter you from side to side, up and down, until you're so dizzy, you can't walk straight when it stops. Mom was supposed to be telling me the truth, correcting Rona Cummins's lies—like plain old, reliable gravity after a wild roller coaster. But now it was Mom's story that I couldn't believe, Mom who sounded crazy.

"Right," I said, hiding behind sarcasm. "How silly of me to forget."

Mom didn't answer.

"Come on, Mom," I said. "If I knew these secrets, wouldn't I know that I knew them?"

Finally, Mom looked away from me. She peered down at her hands and spoke so softly that I had to move close to hear.

"What your parents did was like building a system to replicate memory on a computer. But it was human memory they could copy, not digital. I—I didn't understand it. I was just the stupid younger sister, tagging along, asking dumb questions." Mom sounded like she was going to cry again, but she swallowed hard and got her voice under control. "Once they linked a computer system and a human mind, they could pick and choose, enhance some memories, delete others. But Toria said they would never permanently delete a memory. They would just store it on a computer and block it out of the mind."

"So the war veterans didn't remember the war," I said.

"Not on an everyday basis," Mom said. "If they wanted to recall it, they'd have to go to the computer."

Mom's spooky voice was scaring me more than I wanted to admit. And what she was telling me was just too freaky.

"Toria and Alexei had lots of ethical concerns about their inventions. They wondered if it was right to give some people virtually unlimited capacities for memory. And they worried about people being forced to forget memories they wanted to keep," Mom said. "They were terrified of what Rona Cummins kept calling 'commercial applications.'"

"What does she want to do? Sell this stuff at the grocery?"

Mom shrugged. "I'm not entirely sure. But in the wrong hands . . . What if the British forced the Irish to forget their years of strife? What if the Israelis made the Palestinians forget that they have any claim to the Holy Land? Or, conversely, what if the Palestinians gave the Israelis the same kind of amnesia?"

"Hey, maybe everyone would stop fighting," I said.

"It's not that easy," Mom said. "All those people would lose their identity. *I* think they'd fight more."

I frowned, my head spinning. I didn't want to think about all the problems my parents' inventions could unleash on the world.

"Mom, honest," I said, "I don't know anything about this stuff. Remember? I barely squeaked by with a B minus in computer class last year. And that was because Lynne helped me."

Mom was back to giving me her earnest gaze. She'd looked me straight in the eye more in the past fifteen minutes than she had in the previous thirteen years.

"Before I took you from Crythe," she said slowly, "your parents implanted what they called a 'memory chip' in your brain. It held copies of both of their memories. They wanted you to be able to understand, when you were older. . . . They hypnotized you so you'd have no access to the memories until then. You only need to be hypnotized and told to seek out those memories, and then you'll know everything."

I shook my head, not wanting to accept what she was telling me. Automatically, I reached up and touched my scalp, my fingers searching through my hair. I didn't know what I was looking for. A scar? A USB port?

Mom put her hand over mine, stopping me.

"You can't feel it now," she said. "It's all inside, embedded in your brain. Everything external healed over a long time ago."

Mom was looking at me kindly—even lovingly—but she made me feel like a freak, some sort of cyber-monster my parents had cobbled together.

"When were you planning on telling me all this?" I asked angrily.

"In the beginning I wasn't sure. When you were a toddler, I thought fifteen, sixteen, seventeen was old enough. I thought I'd recognize the right time when it came. I didn't want to keep the secret all by myself forever. I wanted . . . company. But then we put down roots in Willistown. We weren't Crythian anymore. You were like all the other kids. These last few years I was beginning to think . . . never. You didn't ever need to

know anything. What good would those memories do you?"

I was torn between fury and relief. Mom was
right. I hadn't even known those memories were
in my head, and already they'd caused me a world
of trouble. And yet—I had longed to know more
about my father, about where I'd come from. A lot
about Mom and me that I'd never understood was
beginning to make sense now. I wanted everything to make sense.

"No wonder you were so upset about my
friends hypnotizing me," I muttered. I remembered my mother's words on Saturday: "So it will
happen." She'd meant that I would remember
everything after all. I had to tell her how wrong
she was. "But they didn't make me remember any
of my parents' memories. Just my own."

Already I was racking my brain, searching the
dark recesses of my mind for some hint of a memory that wasn't entirely mine. But there was nothing there, nothing I hadn't experienced or seen or
heard or read or dreamed up all by myself.

Mom could tell what I was doing.

"Don't try to remember," she said. "You can't
unless you're hypnotized. And it's too dangerous.
If they even suspect you have the secrets—"

"The Crythians don't know?" I said. "Rona
doesn't?"

Mom shook her head.

"No, thank God," she said. "They never would have even known where we were if I hadn't tried to find out about them. After you were asking me all those questions, I got curious. I was afraid all your memories might, um, surface, and I wanted to know how things stood back in Crythe. Just in case. I took a leave of absence from the library. I was going to be Sophia Landon, ace detective."

"You were going to come back here?" I asked. "To spy?"

"Nooo, probably not," Mom said slowly. "I didn't want to go anywhere unless I had to. I just wanted . . . time to think."

Yep, that's Mom. She'd take a month off work just for time to think.

She kept talking.

"I did a few computer searches at the library. I thought I was discreet, but I guess I'm too much of an amateur." She looked around wildly, as if remembering all over again that her mistakes had led us to this horrible concrete cell. "I might as well have sent out flares," she said bitterly.

"Mom, don't be so hard on yourself," I said. I wanted to comfort her, but I couldn't think of anything to say. I was still in shock myself. Then I remembered we didn't have to be hopeless. "Oh, I almost forgot—Lynne went out to get help.

She'll tell the police where we are, and they'll come and get us. Don't worry. Everything will be all right!"

Mom looked at me like I'd totally lost all my senses.

"Lynne?" she said.

And then I explained about Lynne stowing away in my suitcase, and hiding under the bed, and escaping when I went out to give the speech. When I finished, Mom looked almost hopeful.

"Well, you're right, maybe we do have a shot at being rescued," she said. "That Lynne can be very convincing."

"Yes, she sure can," I said excitedly. I looked back at the door, as if expecting to see it open any minute. The gray walls around me didn't look nearly so grim anymore. "And she's smart, too," I bragged. "*She* should be the Crythian, not me."

"Oh, Crythians aren't smart," Mom said. "You don't understand. Having a good memory isn't the same as intelligence. Intelligence involves insight, being able to make connections, solve problems. If anything, Crythians' memories get in the way of their intelligence. Except for your parents, the rest of us were always too busy trying to keep track of our memories to truly understand anything. We don't really think very well."

I thought again about how all the people had

watched me during my speech. They *had* seemed almost stupid, staring and staring. I closed my eyes, trying to make sense of everything Mom had told me. My mind kept skirting the biggest revelation she'd made, about the secrets stashed away in my own head. No matter how much I'd wondered about my parents, I didn't want their memories in my brain. That made me something else: not just plain old Kira Landon from Willistown, Ohio, but a freak of nature, a mutant, a—a—I didn't even know if there was a term for something like me.

Regardless of what you called someone with a computer chip and other people's memories in her head, that wasn't what I wanted to be. And I sure didn't want anyone else to know what I was.

"If Lynne rescues us," I began. "No—I mean, *when* she rescues us—the Crythians won't be able to accuse us of anything, will they? I mean, there's no way they could guess that I—"

Mom sat up straight.

"Absolutely not," she snapped. "Your parents never told anyone but me what they did. And I haven't told Rona or her cronies a thing. Not since they came and got me, right after you left for school. Come to think of it, they were probably watching to make sure you were gone before they got me. . . . Rona showed no interest in you until I refused to cooperate. I thought I could just drop a note behind me and you'd be safe at Lynne's house."

"Mom, I can't drive," I reminded her.

"I was trying . . . Oh, never mind," Mom said. I noticed she wouldn't look me in the eye. She shook her head angrily. "That Rona is so despicable! I don't know how she's managed to get all of Crythe under her power. Or maybe she doesn't have complete control, if she thought she had to use you to manipulate them. . . . I'm so glad you showed her that *you* weren't going to be one of her pawns!"

Mom sounded proud. I wasn't sure I'd ever done anything to make Mom sound so proud.

I thought about how differently Mom and I had been treated.

"Have they, uh, fed you?" I asked hesitantly.

"No," Mom said. "Not since I got here. But I don't know how long ago that was. They knocked me out at our place, and I woke up here. What day is it, anyway? What time is it?"

"Thursday," I said. That was the only question I could answer with certainty. It seemed like the day had already lasted several lifetimes, but I remembered that the sun had barely been over the horizon when I'd given my speech to the Crythians. Of course, with the difference in time zones, Lynne and I had probably awakened incredibly early, West Coast time. "I guess it's still Thursday morning," I told Mom in amazement.

"Then Rona or her cronies were in here harassing me practically every hour through the night," Mom said bitterly. "I thought she was just doing that again when you opened the door. That's why I pretended to be sleeping."

So Mom hadn't eaten in more than a day, and she'd had a night of constantly interrupted sleep on a cold concrete floor, and she was still looking at me like *I* was the one she was really worried about. I suddenly wished I could give Mom even one of those apples I'd rolled under the bed for Lynne.

But Lynne had needed all the energy she could get, I reminded myself, because she was going to save us all.

It was then that I heard footsteps outside the door.

Twenty-Four

I POKED MOM IN THE SIDE, AND WE BOTH SPRANG BACK from the door. We watched it unblinkingly. We heard a key in the door, saw the handle turning. . . .

"Oh, please, let it be Lynne," I murmured. "Please."

I willed myself to see Lynne's familiar face beaming at me; my ears waited to hear, *Oh, there you are!*

The door opened.

And—yes! I saw Lynne's brown hair first, the strands that always escaped from her ponytail sticking out on the side. I was already on my feet, ready to race to her in glee and relief, my mouth already braced to scream, *You found us!*

Then the door opened the rest of the way, and I saw her face. I froze.

There was not a shred of joy in Lynne's expression, only terror. Her teeth were clenched, her eyes bugged out; she seemed seconds away from releasing the kind of endless shrieks I'd heard only in horror movies. I couldn't stand to keep looking. I peered beyond her. Foolishly, I still held some hope that some California police officer would be on her heels, come to release us.

Rona Cummins stood behind her.

Wildly, I looked over at Mom, wanting to signal her with my eyes. There were three of us and only one of the enemy. We could overpower her....

Mom was staring at something between the Cummins woman and Lynne. Lynne turned slightly, and then I saw it too.

A gun. Mom was staring at the gun wedged against Lynne's back.

"This is all you need to see," Rona Cummins said. "Just in case you had any wild delusions about counting on this one for help." She reached out as though she was going to shut the door again.

Mom stuck her foot in the door.

"That girl is an innocent bystander," she said with incredible calm. "Let her go."

Rona raised an eyebrow.

"Oh, so you can speak," she said. "But I'm sorry, I'll have to deny your only request. How stupid do you think I am?"

"Her parents are undoubtedly looking for

her," Mom said, still with that even, measured voice. "No one's looking for Kira or me. If you take her home, we can settle this peacefully. Just us."

Rona laughed.

"You have some nerve," she said. I wondered how I ever could have trusted her. How desperate had I been? She was still talking. "You think I'm going to bargain? Negotiate? I'm holding all the chips."

"Are you?" Mom said quietly.

"Am I?" Rona repeated. She was gripping Lynne's arm so tightly that her hand might as well have been a tourniquet. "Are you trying to tell me something? Do you have anything to trade for this 'innocent bystander's' life?"

Mom didn't say anything.

"Maybe you need to be convinced that you should tell me something," Rona said. She pressed the gun deeper into Lynne's back. Lynne winced. Rona smiled, a nasty, heartless, reptilian smile. "I have reasons to keep you and Kira alive right now. I don't need this girl. And"—now she looked directly at me—"yes, my little friend, *this* is what's known as blackmail."

I looked at Lynne, to see how she was taking all this. She yelped just a bit, and I thought that that was amazingly brave of her. I would have screamed. Then I saw that Lynne was swaying a little, like she might faint. She reached out and grabbed the door for support.

"Give us some time," Mom begged frantically. She wasn't even trying to sound calm anymore.

"There's not much time left," Rona said, and she jerked Lynne toward her. Lynne was still holding on to the door, so the motion pulled the door back. Lynne let go only seconds before the door shut.

And then I saw that Lynne had not just been holding on to the door to keep herself from fainting. She'd been sticking a scrap of paper there.

Twenty-Five

I PULLED THE PAPER FROM THE BACK OF THE DOOR. Lynne had attached it with chewing gum.

"See how smart Lynne is?" I told Mom proudly.

I unfolded the small square, which was just paper torn from one of Lynne's school notebooks. Of course—she'd had her backpack with her when she hid in the trunk of the car.

The note said:

> *Crythe is a ghost town. Except for the main street and the castle we're in, it's all in ruins. And I'm pretty sure some of the Crythians are actors.*

Then, in big, emphatic writing, she'd added:

DON'T TRUST AUNT MEMORY!

"Thanks a lot," I muttered. "Don't you think I already figured that out?"

"She probably wrote that before she was caught," Mom said distractedly.

I had a sudden chill. I could just picture Lynne sneaking back into my room, trying to warn me before she went for help. What if that was the reason she got caught?

I made myself focus on the rest of the note.

"Crythe's a ghost town, and the people are just actors," I muttered. "Does that mean everything here is just a—a fraud?"

"It didn't used to be," Mom said. "But in the war . . . a lot of the village was destroyed. Rona must have repaired just enough to make it look good, and perhaps she hired extra 'villagers.'" She squinted off into space, deep in thought. "At least some of the original Crythians must still be here, or Rona wouldn't have gone through that charade with the ceremonial dress. I don't know how to think about all of this. . . . Was she trying to trick you and them both? Does she suspect that some of them know more about your parents' invention than they've let on? And she thought you might get them to tell?"

I sank to the floor.

"We don't know anything," I said.

Mom whirled around. She kicked the wall.

"We know this is real," she said. "So was that gun."

I swallowed hard.

"She's not going to kill Lynne, is she?" I asked in a shaky voice.

"We have to have a plan," Mom said. "There must be some way to rescue you and Lynne without betraying the entire world."

I didn't think about it until later, how Mom hadn't included herself in the list of people who needed to be rescued.

Mom sat down by the door again, her chin on her knees, her face in her hands.

"I have to be able to think," she mumbled. "I'm not good at plans. If only Toria and Alexei were here . . ."

A chill traveled down my spine.

"They can be," I said slowly. I could barely bring myself to say the words. "If you hypnotized me and gave me access to their memories, wouldn't it be just like—"

"No!" Mom shouted. She'd never shouted at me like that before. I stared at her and she stared back. "Anything but that," Mom added, only a little less vehemently. "Everything Rona has done proves that your parents' memories should not be . . . resurrected. I have to protect you from that. Protect the rest of the world. No, we have to trick Rona, make her believe we're going to give her the secrets, and then make sure you and Lynne are safe before she finds out the truth. . . . Oh, if only I could think of something!"

I didn't want Mom to see how relieved I was that she didn't expect me to be hypnotized, become my parents. I hunched over and shoved my hands into my pockets. That's when I felt the keys I'd put there the day before and had totally forgotten until now. I pulled them out, one from each pocket.

"Mom, look," I said, feeling a sudden thrill. "Maybe . . ." I didn't have a complete plan formed in my head, but something was coming together. I looked down at the tag on the first key: SAFE-DEPOSIT BOX, FIRST BANK OF WILLISTOWN. I held it out to Mom.

"Where did you get this?" Mom asked.

"From the kitchen cabinet, back home," I admitted. "When you wouldn't answer any of my questions, I thought . . ." It all seemed so long ago. Now I couldn't imagine being so naive that I believed I could get answers from a lockbox. "Never mind what I thought. What if we tell Rona that the secrets are stored at the bank?"

"But they aren't," Mom said. "As soon as she

sees they're not there, she'll just be right back at us, madder than ever. She'll kill Lynne without a single qualm."

I shivered, not wanting to be reminded how high the stakes were.

"No, Mom, she can't open your lockbox," I said. "Nobody can but the person who owns it. The bank people won't let her. I—" I couldn't look Mom in the face. "Lynne and I called the bank to find out what their rules were, and they told us. So you'll have to go with her back to Willistown and to the bank. You can tell her you won't go without me and Lynne. And then when we get there, we can tell the security guard, and they'll call the cops."

I could see a few problems with that plan— like, wouldn't Rona figure out that we could turn her in once we got to the bank? I looked back up at Mom, wondering if she'd shoot down the whole idea.

"That just might work," Mom said slowly. "Except . . . we'll have to tell Rona that the lockbox is in your name."

"What?" I said, suddenly confused.

Now it was Mom's turn to avoid my eyes.

"It's better that way," she said. "Safer."

Twenty-Six

WHEN RONA CUMMINS CAME BACK, MOM MET HER at the door.

"We have a deal to offer you," Mom said in a dull voice, her eyes trained on the floor.

I stood a few paces behind her, where Mom had told me to stand. Mom had scripted the whole thing. I felt like a little kid again, just obeying my mother, without a single thought in my own head.

"A deal?" Rona's eyes glinted with interest. "So you've come to your senses after all."

"You didn't leave us many choices," Mom said, still in the emotionless tone of someone who is either drugged or deeply depressed.

"Well, let's hear it," Rona said eagerly.

"All my sister and brother-in-law's notes on their, um, experiments are in a bank vault back in Ohio," Mom said. "Kira has the key."

This was my cue. I reached into my pocket with what was supposed to be a dramatic flourish. I'm not sure I carried it off. I was so nervous, my hands shook. When I pulled the key free from my pocket, it swung on its ring like a miniature pendulum.

"I knew there was a reason to kidnap you!" Rona chortled. "Hand it over."

She reached out, as if it had never occurred to her that I wouldn't automatically do as she said.

At the last minute, just before her hand brushed mine, I pulled the key away and stuffed it back into my pocket.

"Not so fast," Mom cautioned.

But Rona's reflexes were lightning quick. In the time it took me to blink once, Rona had pulled out her gun and had it pointed at my head.

"I said, hand it over!" Rona commanded.

It was a weird thing to have a gun pointed at me. I've seen people point guns all the time in movies or on TV at my friends' houses. But it's different when it's my head the gun is aimed at, my life that's only seconds away from being extinguished.

I heard Mom gulp. She stepped between me and the gun.

"I said we had a deal, not a giveaway," she told Rona. I hoped I was the only one who heard the quiver in her voice. "That key won't do you any good without Kira."

Rona squinted at Mom. Mom kept talking.

"The safe-deposit box is in Kira's name," Mom said. "She has to sign at the bank to have it opened. Only she can remove any of the contents."

Mom's voice was definitely shaking now. I hoped Rona thought it was just because she was scared. What if she guessed that Mom was lying?

"Come on, then, Kira," Rona said, motioning me toward her with the gun.

"You take all three of us," Mom said. "Me, Kira, Kira's friend. Take us back to Willistown. We open the safe-deposit box, you take everything that's inside it, you set us free."

"You have it all figured out, don't you?" Rona growled. "I think you have a little bit too much figured out. No. I'm taking just Kira. You and the other girl will stay here. That way, she'll have some incentive to play this straight. Any tricks and . . ." Rona squeezed the trigger. I screamed, terrified that, any second now, a bullet would rip through Mom or me. Maybe both of us. But at the last minute Rona had pulled the gun to the side, shot into the wall.

Rona laughed gleefully.

"Scared you, huh?" she taunted us.

"That was dangerous," Mom said. Her face was

white and angry. "Bullets can ricochet. You might have killed any of us."

"I just wanted you to know I was serious," Rona said.

"So am I," Mom said. "You take Kira and Lynne both. If you have to have a hostage, you can keep me here until you have the secrets. Then you release me, too. Deal?"

I gasped. What was Mom thinking? Rona would kill her for sure when she discovered there were no secrets in the lockbox.

Rona glanced my way, and I struggled to regain my poker face. *Rona mustn't suspect, she mustn't suspect,* I repeated to myself again and again. I didn't let myself think anything else.

Rona narrowed her eyes and studied my face even more carefully than ever before.

"You're scaring me with that gun," I muttered, trying to sound childish. I had to make myself seem like a stupid girl who knew nothing about secrets or secret plans, who was merely terrified out of her wits.

I must have succeeded. Rona turned her attention back to Mom.

"Deal?" Mom repeated. Her jaw was set, her eyes blazing. I wondered that I had ever considered her mousy.

"All right," Rona said. "Come on, kid." She

reached out to grab my elbow, and I was too stupefied to pull away.

"Mom?" I said weakly.

"Everything will be fine," Mom said in that reassuring mother voice that I'd heard plenty of other kids' mothers use, but never Mom. Never before that morning. "Just do what we talked about."

Rona looked suspiciously from me to Mom.

"You try any funny stuff, kid, and your so-called mother here is a dead woman," Rona said threateningly. "So are you and your friend."

"You can't hurt the girls," Mom said firmly. "The bank has instructions to destroy the contents of that box in the event of Kira's death."

Nice bluff, I thought. Mom spoke so convincingly, I could almost imagine reams of secret papers going up in smoke. I wished there really were papers, instead of blocked-off information in my brain. And I wished I could figure out the full extent of Mom's plan. I tried to catch Mom's eye, but she was looking past me. She grabbed me by the shoulders and wrapped her arms around my back. She buried her face in my hair.

"Don't worry about me," she whispered into my ear. "There had to be a sacrificial lamb."

Rona pulled me away from Mom.

"Hey, hey, none of that," she said. "Come on."

She pressed the gun into my back and steered me out the door. The feel of the cold metal through my shirt made me so terrified, I didn't even say good-bye to Mom.

Twenty-Seven

I WAS AFRAID THAT RONA WOULD RENEGE ON HER side of the bargain right away and try to leave without Lynne. And then, without Mom, I would have to stand up to Rona all by myself. Would I be able to do that? I didn't think so. Because if I could, I would be digging my heels in right now, screaming, *I'm not leaving Crythe without Mom!*

Except Mom had said for me to go. She had told me not to worry about her.

Dazed, I crossed the basement and climbed the stairs. I was barely aware of anything around me except the gun jabbing into my back.

Just outside the kitchen, Rona directed me to a door I hadn't noticed before. I opened it. It was a small closet, empty except for Lynne's unconscious form on the floor. She lay curled into a fetal position, her long brown hair covering her face. Her school backpack was still strapped to her back, and somehow that made everything worse.

"If you hurt her . . ." I said, trying desperately for the threatening tone Mom had used.

"Relax," Rona said. "We only gave her a mild sedative. For her own good. She was getting hysterical."

I tried to imagine Lynne hysterical but couldn't.

Rona gave Lynne a soft kick, and Lynne moaned and rolled over. I saw that her arms and legs were bound. She opened her eyes. As soon as she saw me, she struggled to sit up.

"Kneel," Rona commanded me.

Seconds later Lynne and I were handcuffed together, her right wrist and my left one. Then Rona took a rope and tied our ankles together too. She grunted in satisfaction when she was done.

"That way, one bullet will stop both of you," she said.

"Three-legged race," Lynne whispered in my ear.

I knew what she meant. Lynne and I had been partners at lots of birthday parties and Sunday school picnics and end-of-school class day relay races when we were little kids—she thought we could make a break for it.

I shook my head warningly.

"They still have Mom," I whispered back.

Lynne's eyes got big, and she frowned questioningly.

"We have a deal," I said, loud enough for Rona to hear. She was probably eavesdropping anyhow. "Rona here is flying you and me back to Willistown so we can get some important papers out of *my* lockbox." I only dared to emphasize the "my" a little bit. I hoped Lynne picked up on it. "Then she's going to set us free. And Mom, too."

"*If* the papers are what I need," Rona said. "*If* you don't try to sabotage the deal. *If* everything goes my way."

"It will," I said in my best good-girl voice. I suddenly wished I'd had more experience lying. I didn't think I sounded very confident. But it's hard to sound that way with a gun in your back.

"What are the papers?" Lynne asked as casually as if she were making sure of a homework assignment. *She* knew I was lying, I thought. And Lynne was crafty enough to try to distract Rona.

"Don't you worry about that," Rona snapped. "The less you know, the more likely you are to get out of this alive."

I swallowed hard, too worried to try to cover my panic anymore. How were we going to get out of this alive? The plan Mom and I had talked about depended on us being able to get help from a security guard at the bank before the lockbox was opened. But no security guard in the First Bank of Willistown could save Mom if she wasn't there with us.

Rona had known that, I realized. That was why she'd agreed to take Lynne but had made Mom stay behind.

But why had Mom agreed?

Rona gave me a shove, and Lynne and I both stumbled. I realized I'd missed a command.

"She's taking us to the plane," Lynne hissed.

I nodded and numbly went along. At the front door Rona paused and spoke to a uniformed man. It was a long conversation, and when it was done, Rona turned to me.

"If he does not hear good news from me by eight o'clock tonight," she said, "he will kill Sophia. Does that motivate you a little more?"

My heart pounded. I could only nod.

We went out the front door and got into the same car we'd ridden in the night before. A different uniformed man drove; Rona sat in the front and watched Lynne and me. Lynne tapped my foot with her shoe, as if we could communicate that way. Lynne was probably trying Morse code or something like that; Lynne probably actually knew Morse code. I didn't. I scowled at Lynne, the universal sign for, *Leave me alone. I'm thinking*.

Lynne's face crumbled, and I reminded myself

that Lynne wasn't exactly having a festive time herself. She stopped tapping my foot and turned her head to stare out the window.

"I'm sorry," I whispered, but I don't think she heard.

We arrived at what must have been the same field we'd flown to the night before. By daylight it looked even smaller and more isolated, just one long strip of concrete runway in the midst of overgrown brush. Off to the side there was a falling-down shack that must have been the airport office. Our pilot from the night before limped out from that shack.

"Khahy!" Rona yelled at him as soon as the car stopped. He came over and there was yet another long conversation among Rona, our pilot, and our driver. The flow of words made my head ache. I tried to tune it out. Lynne leaned over to me.

"I think one of their verb tenses is a variation on the syllable 'sta,'" she whispered out of the side of her mouth. "They keep repeating that. Do you understand anything?"

I looked over, and Lynne was squinting in concentration, as if she were going to become fluent in Crythian if she listened for just another two or three minutes. She was trying so hard, I couldn't stand it. I almost hated Lynne just then. Or maybe I hated myself for not trying.

Before I could answer Lynne, Rona ordered us out of the car and over to the plane. Lynne and I silently climbed into the back. Rona and the two men stayed outside the plane, leaning against the open door, still talking.

"I bet they're arguing about who's going and who's staying," Lynne whispered. "They're not even watching us. Do you think we could start up the plane and leave without them?"

I stared at Lynne in disbelief.

"Do you have any clue how to fly this thing?" I asked her. "You'd kill us for sure. We haven't even taken driver's ed yet. Besides, they'd hear the minute we started the engine. And you can't just take off in one second flat."

Lynne flushed red.

"Okay, so that's not such a hot idea. But what's *your* plan? Why don't you fill me in?"

"We have to—," I started. To my surprise, my eyes filled with tears and my throat closed over before I could continue. I swallowed hard, made myself speak.

"Mom," I said, "wants us to save ourselves and let her die."

Twenty-Eight

I HADN'T FULLY REALIZED THE TRUTH UNTIL I SPOKE IT. Once the words were out of my mouth, I felt faint. My head swam, and Lynne's worried face seemed to recede before my eyes. I couldn't focus on Lynne's response for a long time.

". . . you sure?" she was saying when I finally made my ears hear.

I nodded, the tears flooding my eyes again.

"What Rona wants—," I began. I glanced out the plane door, but Rona and the two men were engrossed in their argument. They couldn't hear me. "It isn't in that lockbox," I whispered. "It's all a bluff. But Mom thinks when we get into the bank, we can tell a security guard and save ourselves. Rona won't expect us to—to betray Mom."

My voice broke on that awful word. "Betray."

Lynne stared at me without blinking. Her face seemed to be all eyes.

"Your mom told you that?" she asked.

"She said, 'Don't worry about me. There had to be a sacrificial lamb.' And you have to understand, the way she looked at me, when she said to just do what we'd talked about . . .'" Mom had known all along that Rona wouldn't take all three of us, I realized. She'd planned the whole negotiation, certain she would have to trade her life for ours.

"Maybe Rona's bluffing too," Lynne said. "She wouldn't really kill your mom, would she? What are the papers she wants, anyhow?"

I hesitated. Part of me ached to tell Lynne the whole story. I didn't want the burden of it entirely on my shoulders. But Lynne had started treating me differently when she suspected I was a refugee—what would she think of me when she found out the rest of my secrets? Maybe she wouldn't even believe me.

And how could telling possibly help Mom?

I looked around desperately. The backseat of the plane was so small, I felt trapped. Just a few feet away Rona's argument with the two men had escalated. They were shouting at one another now. I saw the man who'd driven our car shove the pilot back against the door to the plane. He winced with pain, and Rona immediately began yelling at the driver.

"Tell me now," Lynne urged. "They aren't listening to us at all."

But I was watching Rona. She raised her arm, and the sun flashed on the gun she'd been pointing at Lynne and me all morning. The driver backed away. I saw Rona squeeze the trigger, and the gunshot echoed throughout the clearing. But the driver wasn't hit. He took off running, straight for the deep woods around us.

"That was your warning!" Rona yelled after him. "I missed on purpose, you fool!"

She glanced over at Lynne and me. I realized that she'd spoken in English solely for our benefit.

"She— She's not in control," Lynne whispered to me as soon as Rona looked away. "She's trigger-happy and she's not in control."

I was amazed that Lynne could analyze the situation so calmly. Then I saw that her teeth were chattering with fear; her face was as white as her T-shirt.

Both of us knew that Rona hadn't missed on purpose.

Rona and Jacques were climbing into the front of the plane now, shutting the doors. Rona turned and faced Lynne and me.

"I don't want any funny business out of the two of you," she snapped. "I'm done giving warnings.

Next time, I just shoot. Both of you are expendable as far as I'm concerned."

I should have objected, reminded her that she couldn't get into the lockbox without me. But I could still see her squeezing the trigger, could still hear the gunshot ringing in my ears. I was paralyzed.

She seemed to know what I was going to say anyway.

"Now that I know where it is, I'll have no problem getting what I want out of that safe-deposit box. I have some experience robbing banks—did I tell you that?" Rona asked. "It's just easier using you. If you cooperate."

She's crazy, I thought.

I didn't need Lynne to figure that one out for me.

The pilot closed both doors, checked his instruments, and began preparing for flight.

This can't be happening, I thought.

I squeezed my eyes shut. When I opened them, we were speeding down the runway. And then we were flying, rising, rising, over trees, over mountains. Ignoring the pressure building in my ears, I peered out the window, searching for Crythe. I could see no sign of it. The village must have been behind us. It didn't matter. I knew that with every second we spent in the air, we got farther and farther from Mom.

Twenty-Nine

IT'S A LONG WAY FROM CALIFORNIA TO OHIO.

That's one of those facts I had never fully appreciated sitting in a classroom, staring at a map of the United States. And I hadn't noticed on the flight out because I'd been unconscious most of the way from Willistown to Crythe.

But now, sitting in that little plane with a lunatic, an old man, and my frightened best friend, I found every second excruciating. I wanted to talk to Lynne, but Rona kept turning around and peering at us with her beady eyes.

Why hadn't I noticed yesterday how deranged she looked? How bitter the lines were around her mouth, how greedily her eyes glowed, how coldly she surveyed all around her?

Obviously, I wasn't much of a judge of character. Or I'd been even more blinded than I'd thought.

When we'd been in the air for about half an hour, Lynne started giggling beside me. Rona immediately snapped her head back to glare at her. I stared too.

"Peanuts," Lynne said between giggles. "I was just thinking that if we were on a commercial flight, they'd be bringing us peanuts right about now. Or pretzels. And they'd ask if we want Coke or Sprite. . . . Isn't that funny?"

Her voice sounded high and strange over the plane's noises. Her giggles floated out like something entirely separate from her body.

Rona leveled the gun against the seat back. She was aiming at a spot between Lynne's eyes.

"Stop laughing," Rona commanded. "Now."

Lynne stopped.

A minute later, as soon as I dared to look over at Lynne again, she had tears streaming down her face. She was sobbing in absolute silence.

Now Lynne was losing it too.

I patted Lynne's shoulder, but she didn't even seem to notice.

I couldn't worry about Lynne. She and I were going to be okay. There was still hope for us. But Mom . . .

Just thinking about Mom made me feel like I was standing on a sandy beach and waves kept knocking me down and sweeping the sand away.

Every time I tried to get back up on solid ground, I'd find there was no solid ground within reach. I just kept tumbling over and over again, drowning in memory.

When Mom and I were locked in that basement room together, before Rona came back and Mom made her deal, Mom had started reminiscing.

"I don't think I've been much of a mother to you," she'd apologized. "But I want you to know, I did my best."

She'd talked about being a naive Crythian peasant, cast out in a strange land.

"I knew I had to get far away from Crythe," she said. "But that trip across America was torture. All those neon signs burned into my memory. . . . I'd pull off the road at night and curl up with you in the car and try to sleep, try to forget—anything. All I could do was cry. I didn't even feel like myself anymore. I felt old, because everything in America was new. It seemed like I had to remember it, because it'd be gone the next day. And then I got to Willistown, and it looked old and unchanging. All those Victorian houses on Maple Street, you know? They looked like they'd lasted. Like you could hide in them and not be scared, because they'd withstood a lot and were bound to withstand a lot more. And they would keep standing. I went to the library, because for the first time I wanted to know more about a place we were passing through. And within an hour, Mrs. Steele had offered me a job and a place to live.

"I know I was strange in Willistown. I know you probably suffered for that. But I didn't know how not to be Crythian. I couldn't have bought a TV and let it go blaring in my house night and day, like your friends had. I couldn't make small talk with all the neighbors and try not to remember every 'Hi' and 'How are you?' for the rest of my days. I couldn't let go of my memories of Toria and Alexei, my mama and papa, Crythe. I couldn't change. I could only . . . let you be different."

Mom's eyes had looked liquid, like twin pools of memory and regret.

"We could have hidden better in a big city," she'd said. "I know that now. We could have been anonymous, unnoticed. But Willistown was my gift to you. A normal place to grow up. A place for you to become a normal person."

I hadn't known what to say. I'd just stared at her, still trying to piece everything together. All those "Hi's" and "How are you?'s" our neighbors had spoken back in Willistown had been like bridges, foundations for the real sharing that went beyond small talk. But Mom and I had never had those connections. She was still a stranger to me. But a stranger who mattered more to me than my closest friends. She had risked her life for me all those years ago, and she was ready to sacrifice her life for me now.

I couldn't let her do it.

I'm not going to let Mom die, I thought, and that fierce certainty was solid ground at last.

Calculatingly, I looked around the tiny plane cabin. I was like Lynne, before, full of wild ideas: The pilot was old—could we overpower him? Could one of us get the gun away from Rona? Were there parachutes for us to escape in? I'd never touched a parachute in my life, but I could imagine floating down, calling the police, storming Crythe long before eight o'clock that night.

I might as well have imagined a white horse and a knight in shining armor. My wild ideas were every bit as useless as Lynne's had been.

Lynne was still sobbing beside me, and I felt close to despair myself. Sure, I was determined to save Mom, but that didn't do any good if I didn't know what to do.

And then, out of nowhere, I did know.

Thirty

I JOSTLED LYNNE'S FOOT WITH MY TOE. WHEN THAT didn't work, I kicked her ankle.

"Ou—" She swallowed a yelp of pain, but Rona looked back suspiciously at us anyhow.

"What's going on back there?" Rona growled.

"Um, nothing," I said quickly. "You wouldn't mind if we went to sleep, would you?"

Rona gazed at us with narrowed eyes, then seemed to decide sleep was harmless.

"Be my guest," she said, smiling at the irony of her words.

I motioned to Lynne to lean forward and prop her head against the seats in front of us, just like kids do sleeping on the school bus.

"What are you doing?" Lynne whispered.

I tilted my head back, to see over the seat. Rona's ears were less than a foot from my mouth. Even with the plane's noises, I couldn't be absolutely certain that she wouldn't hear me. And I *had* to be certain.

"Nothing," I said in a louder-than-usual whisper. "Just going to sleep."

Maybe it was just my imagination, but the corner of Rona's mouth I could see seemed to curve up a little—a slight smile of glee at being able to eavesdrop on us.

But behind the seat I grabbed Lynne's hand, being careful not to make the handcuffs clank. Then, with my finger, I began to trace invisible letters into her palm. At first Lynne squinted in confusion, but then she nodded, just a little, not enough to be noticed from the front seat.

H-Y-P, I began. I felt like Anne Sullivan teaching words to Helen Keller. I felt brilliant for thinking of this way to communicate.

When I'd finally finished the important first nine letters, Lynne held up a finger to stop me and stealthily reached behind her back. She struggled silently with something that was out of my sight. Then she brought out a pen and a sheet of paper.

HYPNOTIZE? she wrote in big letters.

I gave her a grimace that could only begin to show my disgust: How could she have let me spell out that whole, tedious word before reminding me she had pen and paper in her backpack? I felt like a fool. I grabbed the pen from her hand and scrawled, *Hypnotize me and tell me to remember everything. Tell me that every part of my brain is now open to me.*

Lynne read my note, and instantly I began scribbling over the letters until every word I'd written was covered over, indecipherable. Only then did I look over at Lynne, who gave me back a puzzled squint.

Why? she mouthed silently. I could tell she was thinking that the full extent of her brain-power would probably be worth a lot more than mine. But she didn't possess my parents' memories, didn't hold in her brain the ticking time bomb that could change the world.

I hesitated for a second, remembering how Mom had protested when I'd suggested to her that I should recover my parents' memories to save us. I wasn't totally certain that remembering could help us; I only knew that I could do nothing without it. And if there was even a chance that I could save Mom, I was going to take it.

I'll tell you later, I wrote to Lynne. *Just don't let them know what we're doing.* I drew an arrow directed toward the front seat of the plane, as if Lynne needed help figuring out who "them" was. And I underlined the word "don't" about six

times. Then, once again, I inked over everything
I'd written.

Lynne gave an almost invisible shrug and
nodded.

Now? she wrote on the paper.

As soon as we have a chance, I wrote back.

Thirty-One

LYNNE AND I BOTH SLUMPED IN OUR SEATS, JERKING back up every few minutes in our best imitations of people trying to sleep in an uncomfortable place. She leaned right for a while as I leaned left; her head bobbed against the front seat while mine slid down against the back. *If we get out of this alive, we both deserve Best Actress Oscars,* I thought dimly, then had to fight not to giggle and ruin everything. Oscars were like peanuts—not the least bit funny unless your life depended on not laughing.

Through half-closed lids, I monitored Rona's every move in the front. I began counting silently between every glance she directed back at us. When I made it to five hundred without having to start over, I silently slid my head toward Lynne's. I felt like I was moving at the rate of an inch an hour. Finally, finally, my head came to rest against Lynne's shoulder. Her head pitched forward, aided by a little turbulence that threw the whole plane up, then down. When she stopped moving, her face was hidden against my hair, her mouth only inches from my ear. I dug my elbow in her side.

"Is it safe?" she whispered.

I made my head bob up and down, hoping anyone looking from the front would believe I was only moving with the plane's rocking.

"Give me your key, then," she whispered again.

It took me a minute to understand, but then I slid my hand in and out of my pocket, pulling forth the car key this time. I slipped the key into Lynne's grasp, and she let it dangle against the seat, out of Rona's sight. Lynne lifted her hand a little, and the key swung back and forth, back and forth.

"Watch that," Lynne whispered. "Don't think about anything except the key."

But it wasn't as easy to empty my mind as it had been the last time I was hypnotized. I'd had nothing on my mind to begin with that Friday night. Now I had to let go of my fear of Rona, my worries about Mom, my confusion about my past, my terror of my parents' minds. That one stupid swinging key couldn't compete at all for my attention. I thought about Mom trying to leave that key for me, trying to give me an escape. I saw Mom's face on that key, Mom's fate hanging in the balance. Mom, Mom, Mom.

"You are getting sleepy," Lynne whispered. "You are letting go."

I wasn't letting go. I couldn't let myself be overtaken by my parents' memories. I couldn't let go of Mom. But I had to let go to save her. . . .

I don't remember what Lynne said after that. The next thing I was aware of was Lynne shaking me.

"Wake up," she said. "I think we're almost there."

I sat up, disoriented. Almost where? My neck was stiff; my arm had gone numb from being pressed against the seat. My head ached. The plane's engine rumbled behind me.

"You've been sleeping for hours," Lynne said. "You even slept through our refueling stop in—I don't know. I guess it was Kansas, someplace."

She sounded resentful, as if I'd been off having a picnic while she'd been facing terror and torture. She even made Kansas sound dangerous. *Refueling stop?* I thought. That meant I'd probably slept through a refueling stop on my flight to California, too. So much was happening that I wasn't aware of. I was so disoriented, I could barely figure out which way was up.

"Well?" Lynne whispered. "Did it work?"

She shouldn't have risked speaking so openly,

I thought crabbily. Rona could turn around at any time. And what did Lynne mean, "Did it work?"

Then I remembered. Tentatively, like someone groping for a light switch in the dark, I searched my mind. *Hello? Toria? Alexei? Anybody there? Anything you might want to tell me?*

Their names must have been the link. In seconds I was overwhelmed with memories. I knew the value of pi to twenty-five digits. I knew Crythian, Russian, German, and French. I knew how to make a human mind into a computer and vice versa. I knew what it was like to be hungry for days on end, in danger of starvation. I knew rocks and fields and mountains I'd never seen.

I knew my parents.

And I knew who Mom really was.

Thirty-Two

I DIDN'T REALIZE I WAS CRYING UNTIL LYNNE LEANED over and whispered, urgently, "What is it? What's wrong?"

I shook my head. Even if I hadn't had Rona to worry about, I wouldn't have been able to utter a word just then.

Everything was so clear, so vivid, as if I had lived it myself. I knew I was still me, Kira Landon, but I had *them* in me too. I latched on to something familiar, the overlap between all of our memories: the room that Toria had carried me to, to send me out into safety.

I knew now that that room was four blocks east and one block south of the stone castle where we lived. The room had once been the home of a family of five, but they were all dead now, killed in the fighting in Crythe. Killed because of Toria and Alexei's discoveries.

Toria felt guilty about that. I could now
remember, from her perspective, how she'd carried me through the streets: The whole way, she'd
been agonizing over the Miloffs' deaths, other
Crythians' deaths, and the deaths she knew were
still to come. But she was also clutching me,
telling me that *I* would be safe, that Mama and
Papa would never let anything bad happen to
their little Kira.

"You're all right. Everything's okay," she
repeated again and again, and she knew she was
saying it to comfort herself as much as her child.

The cobblestones were slippery, and Toria was
glad that it was too dark to tell whether she was
skidding on rainwater or blood. Her shoes were
heavy wooden clogs—peasant wear, not the business pumps she always wore to meet with all the
computer experts. She did not want to be a computer expert anymore; if she had to die, she
would die a peasant.

At last she reached the heavy wood door. She
blinked back tears to smile at her daughter—to
smile at me—and force out a cheerful-sounding
"And here we are! Just the door we wanted!"

But I twisted up my face, and Toria could see
that I was planning to cry myself, that I knew that
something was wrong.

"Shh, shh, none of that," Toria said, a little

sharply. But inside she was proud that I was not so easily fooled. *You're a smart one,* she thought, and then wondered sadly, *and how much pain will that bring you?*

My toddler body weighed her down as she climbed up the stairs. But once inside the room, Toria relaxed a little. Surely we were safe here, for now. Surely no one had followed, no one saw. She paced back and forth on the plain pine floor, until my head drooped to her shoulder, my eyes slid shut, my mouth fell open in sleep. And still Toria stood and swayed, holding me, not wanting to put me down for what might be the very last time.

"Oh, Kira," she said with a sigh.

I knew then how much my mother loved me. I knew it as a toddler, sleeping on her shoulder, and I knew it now, a teenager on a plane in danger.

At last my mother's trance was broken by the sound of the door opening. She cowered against the wall, holding her breath, until she heard a voice call softly, "Toria?"

It was Alexei, her husband, my father. He switched on a flashlight as soon as he shut the door. The glow illuminated only a small space, but it was enough: I could see his face as she saw it, and I could see her face as he saw it. The worry lines that had been etched into their faces the past few years were erased by the dim light. He looked at her and remembered a skipping girl playing in mountains that were now a hemisphere away; she looked at him and remembered a young boy tossing stones in a stream. Alexei was tall and dark, swarthily handsome. He didn't look any more like the photo Mom once showed me of him than a piece of paper looks like a tree. Which wasn't to say that the photo was a fake—it was just too flat, too two-dimensional.

Toria bore a startling resemblance to her sister. I could see that if they'd been any closer in age, they might have been mistaken for identical twins. Toria had the same rope of hair down her back, the same intent eyes, the same firm jaw.

"Everything is ready," Alexei said softly.

"Except us," Toria countered. "How can we? How can we send our only child away?"

"How can we let her die with us?" Alexei let the question hang in the air. "When there's even a chance—"

"But . . ." Toria wanted to argue their fates, defend their lives. She wanted there still to be time to change their minds.

"Sophia will take care of her," Alexei said, and turned away, unable to look at his sleeping child. Because if he did, he would break down and agree with his wife.

Toria gently placed me on the floor and tucked my blanket around me. "Give me the computer," Toria said. "We should get this over with before Sophia gets here."

Alexei pulled a laptop out of his cloak and handed it to his wife. She hit keys quickly, without looking, rapid strings of complicated sequences. Then she stopped.

"There is no way this will endanger her?" she asked.

"We've been over this again and again," Alexei said. "No one will even know, except her and Sophia. But when—I mean, if—we are killed, we'll want our daughter to know...."

I wouldn't have understood if I hadn't had my parents' minds in mine. Not knowing something was worse than torture for them. It was something that had been beat into them, not in Crythe, but in the Soviet camp where they'd spent most of their childhood. They were desperate to save their daughter from ignorance.

Toria ran a wire from the computer to a tiny bare spot on the back of her scalp. Alexei had implanted a computer port on her brain, just as she had installed one on his.

"This always makes me feel like Frankenstein," she muttered, grimacing at the awkwardness of reaching over her shoulder. She looked like a woman doing nothing more startling than pulling a zipper up that last stubborn inch.

But she and Alexei both knew what was about to happen. He moved to her side to help.

"It was the only way for us to survive," he said. And he wasn't talking about the two of them, Toria and Alexei, but all of Crythe.

"And now we're making our daughter a freak too," Toria said coldly.

"It's reversible," Alexei said soothingly. "She'll know how. We'll give her the knowledge, and she can pick out what she wants to keep."

Toria pushed the final key on the computer, and that was the last memory she copied.

I felt bereft, realizing I'd come to the end of my mother's memories, even though she'd given me twenty-four years' worth before that one. It was almost like witnessing her death.

But Toria hadn't died then.

From Alexei's perspective, I could still see her, moving the computer closer to where I lay, pulling out more computer wire. She seemed very businesslike and efficient now that I couldn't see into the turmoil of her mind. But Alexei saw the tears in her eyes as she bent over me, feeling for the port on my brain that my parents had implanted only hours before, when they'd anesthetized me for a particularly long afternoon nap.

They'd designed mine differently from their own: My port would soon be covered over with skin, disappearing as I grew. Theirs were meant to stay accessible for the rest of their lives.

Finally, Toria straightened up.

"Done," she said. "Your turn now."

Alexei frowned.

"Shouldn't Sophia be here by now?" he asked. "The longer we wait, the more dangerous—"

"She'll come," Toria answered. Alexei heard the challenge in her voice: Didn't he trust his sister-in-law? He had nothing against Sophia; it was just that he trusted no one anymore, no one except Toria. After all, he had once trusted Rona Cummins. . . .

Alexei was reaching for the laptop when he heard the dull thud below. He saw his wife stiffen, saw the fear grow in her eyes.

"I'll go check," he said, trying to sound brave. His legs felt rubbery as he descended the stairs; he had to remind himself to breathe. He did not expect to live much longer, but that didn't mean he was eager to die. And his daughter was still up in the room behind him—he couldn't die until she was safe.

"We've made a mess of everything," he muttered.

He reached the door to the street and put his ear to it. The fighting sounded far away, but how could he tell through such thick wood? Gently, he eased the door open. The sound of the scraping hinges echoed in the empty alley. Alexei winced, terrified that someone would hear and come investigate. Cautiously, he peeked out. Nothing.

Then a hand grabbed his ankle.

"Alexei," a woman's voice croaked.

It was his sister-in-law, Sophia. She was lying on the ground. Alexei might have mistaken her body for a pile of filthy rags if she hadn't spoken.

"Save my ... memories," she murmured.

Alexei risked shining the flashlight on her, and he instantly wished he hadn't. She was lying in a pool of blood. He couldn't tell if her wounds were from knives or bullets, but there was one fact he couldn't ignore: She was dying.

"They got me," she managed to say. "I'm ... sorry. Should have been here for ... Kira. So ... sorry. Just ... save my memories. Please. Please save my memories."

Alexei could admire her determination to get to the room, to him and her sister, but at the same time, heartlessly, he worried that she'd left a trail—a trail of blood to lead their enemies directly to them.

"Let's get you inside," he said grimly. "Maybe we can find a bandage."

His suggestion was so ludicrous that Sophia actually laughed.

Alexei pulled Sophia up the stairs, leaving a stream of blood behind them, a zigzag of drops on every step. She wouldn't last much longer.

"My memories," she was still insisting. "Save—"

They reached the room. Toria was standing in the corner with the laptop held high over her head, ready to whack any unwanted intruder. When she saw Sophia, her arms sagged; even her backbone seemed to melt.

"No," she whispered. Her voice rose to a scream. "No! Not her!"

And Alexei understood suddenly that Toria had suggested her sister take Kira for two reasons: so that Kira would be safe, and so that Sophia would be too. And now Sophia was about to die, and it was, once again, Toria and Alexei's fault.

Toria bent beside her sister, pulling off clothing, feeling for wounds. In seconds, her hands were as bloody as her sister's shirt.

"Save . . . ," Sophia managed to say.

"We can't, baby sister," Toria whispered. "Oh, I'm so sorry. We can't."

"In there. My memories." Sophia somehow managed to point to the computer Toria had dropped by her side.

Toria and Alexei looked at each other, hopelessly. Of all the Crythians, Sophia had had the greatest faith in them and their discoveries. He knew it wasn't fair, but Alexei had always regarded his sister-in-law as somewhat simpleminded. Sure, she could memorize anything she was given, from the periodic table to the Los Angeles phone book. But she had none of her sister's flashes of brilliance, none of her sister's insight. Sophia liked flowers and trees. She liked to look at the sky.

What's the point? he wanted to scream at Sophia. *A computer disk is not eternal life. You'll still be dead.* And even more heartless: *Who would ever want your memories but you?*

He said nothing. He bit his lip. *I am shutting down already,* he thought. *I am losing my humanity.*

Toria leaned closer to her sister, gently brushed the hair back from Sophia's face.

"Of course. Of course," she crooned. "That is how we will keep you. Forever."

Numbly, Alexei watched as Toria's fingers raced across the keyboard, deftly copying Sophia's mind into digital memory.

Alexei chafed at the waste of time—why tend to the dying when Kira was still in danger? But at last Toria straightened up.

"She's gone," she said. "I don't think I got it all." Her voice broke. Alexei forgot that he had given up on his own humanity; he rushed to his wife's side and held her in his arms. Over her shoulder he could see me, Kira, still sleeping soundly on the floor.

"You must go, then," he said. "Take the child and go quickly. Before it is too late."

But Toria was still reaching for the computer, fumbling with wires.

"What are you doing?" Alexei demanded.

Toria had the computer linked to her brain once more. Her fingers flew over the keyboard.

"I can't just *leave* Sophia in there," she said. "The computer is so cold. . . . Her memories will be safer in my mind. Like we're putting our memories in Kira's mind." Her hands shook as she reached back to make the final connection. So many tears streamed from her eyes that Alexei wondered if she could see at all.

"Toria, this is madness," Alexei protested, but his wife didn't seem to hear. He watched helplessly as she made the transfer. Grief had clearly swept away the last traces of her reason. What good would it do to store Sophia's memories in Toria's mind when Toria was about to die too? He wondered, suddenly, if all of Crythe was crazy, thinking memory mattered. Mattered enough to die for.

Alexei was ready to forget.

Down below, the door scraped open and shut. Alexei froze. Toria stiffened as well—this sound, at least, had broken through her trance of grief. Both of them looked around frantically.

There was no place to hide. Except for the baby sleeping on a blanket on the floor, the room might as well have been a tomb. It might well become their tomb, as it had already become Sophia's.

But the baby was sleeping on the floor. Alexei could not allow her to die.

"Quick! I've got a plan!" Toria hissed. Alexei was relieved to see the gleam of reason in her eyes again. "Shut off that flashlight. No—wait—don't. Hand it to me. And lie over there beside Kira."

Baffled, Alexei huddled beside his daughter. He heard footsteps on the stairs—whoever had opened the door was climbing the stairs now. He dared to hope that it was someone who sympathized with Alexei and Toria, but that wasn't likely. Most of their compatriots were dead.

"Don't wake Kira!" Toria ordered. She was tugging on her sister's body, straining and pulling until it was right in front of Alexei and the sleeping child. Then she spread out Sophia's skirt and her hair until Alexei and Kira were hidden behind the corpse.

"It's just her body. It's not her. It's not her memories," Toria said again and again, like a mantra. Through the tangle of hair, Alexei saw Toria pull the kerchief from Sophia's head and tie it under her own chin. Then she fell, face first onto her sister's chest, sobbing.

"Toria? Alexei?" a voice called, and Alexei's heart sank. It was Rona.

From his hiding place, Alexei saw a beam of light flash crazily about the room. He saw Toria turn and throw something toward the door. There was a crash, and then the room went dark. Alexei suddenly understood: Toria had used their flashlight to knock Rona's flashlight out of her hand.

He had to admire his wife's aim. But what was she going to do next?

Rona was cursing Toria. "Give me back my flashlight," she demanded. "Give it to me. Now!"

Alexei could hear someone groping around on the floor. He hoped that Toria found the flashlight before Rona did. Or, at the very least, he hoped both flashlights were broken.

"You killed my sister! You killed Toria!" a voice wailed, and it sounded so much like Sophia that Alexei was spooked. In the darkness he poked one finger against the body in front of him—it was already cold with death.

"Oh, well, there's still Alexei to help me," Rona said carelessly. "Where is he?"

Toria's sobbing intensified.

"He—He saw that she was dead and he ran away," she blubbered.

Rona swore. "Why don't they make this easy for me?" she asked. "They've lost. Why keep fighting?"

"Maybe he was looking for you. I don't know," Toria said through her sobs, barely coherent. "Oh, oh—my sister is dead!"

"Oh, shut up," Rona said. "I should kill you, too."

Alexei couldn't believe Rona's callousness. No—he could. He knew what she was capable of. He braced himself to spring up and defend his wife, if he had to. But it was so dark, he didn't know which way to spring. Toria's keening made her easy to locate, but Rona was moving about the room, still groping for a light.

"Go ahead," Toria challenged. "Kill me. I don't want to go on living without my sister." She sounded so convincing, Alexei worried. Was that what she really believed?

"No. You're not worth my time," Rona countered. "Ugh. Get away from me, you filthy piece of vermin. I mean it. You're getting blood on me."

There were sounds of a struggle. As best as Alexei could tell, Toria must have thrown herself against Rona. A body hit the floor. Alexei dared to hope—

"Serves you right," Rona said. Her footsteps drew closer to the spot where Alexei and Kira lay behind the corpse. Then she paused. "Oh, forget the flashlight."

The footsteps echoed down the stairs.

As soon as he heard the door below, Alexei shoved Sophia's body aside.

"Toria?" he whispered.

She moaned, and that led him to her. On the way he stumbled over a flashlight. He scooped it up, switched it on.

"Are you all right?" he asked, bending at his wife's side.

"I think I . . . hit my head," she mumbled. "Hurts."

Alexei gently turned her head to the side, felt for a wound at the back. The skin wasn't broken, but a small lump was growing right beside the computer port.

"It doesn't look too bad," he assured her. "Oh, Toria, you were incredible. You really fooled her! If I hadn't known, even I would have believed—"

"Toria?" She furrowed her brow in confusion. "What's wrong with you, Alexei? Can't you tell the difference between your wife and your sister-in-law?"

"Come on, Toria, Rona's gone. You don't have to pretend anymore," Alexei said.

"Pretend?" Toria looked even more puzzled. "Who's pretending? I'm not Toria. I'm Sophia."

"No, no, you just bumped your head. You're confused," Alexei insisted.

But even as he spoke the words, he knew. He could recall exact passages from psychology texts that he and Toria had pored over, planning their inventions. It had been dangerous for Toria to bring Sophia's memories into her own mind. The bump on her head was all she needed to lose track of which identity was really hers.

"Sophia?" he said tentatively.

"Yes, of course. Who else?" Toria replied. She struggled to sit up. "You were really scaring me there, Alexei. Where is Toria, anyway? And Kira, I came to get Kira. . . ." She rubbed her forehead. "That's funny. I don't remember coming here. What's wrong with me?"

"You just bumped your head," Alexei repeated, trying to hide his own fear.

"Toria will know—I have to see Toria—"

"She already left. She couldn't bear to say good-bye," Alexei lied frantically. Anything to keep Toria calm.

Toria shook her head, her expression blank— as blank as Sophia's would have been.

"I was in my room, getting ready. And then I was here. How could I forget everything in between? And Toria." Her voice arced toward hysteria.

"Don't worry," Alexei said soothingly. But his mind was running like a rat in a maze. He had to cure his wife— He had to divert Rona before she came back and discovered the truth— He had to protect his daughter—"You'll remember every-thing again, soon," he murmured. But he didn't believe it.

And did he want her to remember Sophia's death?

Toria was turning her head. In a second she would see the corpse of the real Sophia, lying on the floor only a few feet away.

Alexei snapped the flashlight off.

"Alexei!" Toria protested. "I can't see!" And, again, in the darkness, she sounded so completely like Sophia that Alexei doubted his own memory. Toria *was* alive, though she wouldn't be for much longer.

Grimly, Alexei pictured the inevitable future: Either he and Toria would have to reveal their secrets to Rona, or the other Crythians would kill them. And without Sophia to rescue her, Kira would die too.

But Toria could take the baby. She thought she was Sophia anyhow—why not let her go like that?

Alexei saw everything 'itting together. It was *good* that Toria was confused. This way, he could save his wife and his child both. And if he was wrong, if he survived too, he could go after them, restore Toria's true memory, have his family back safe and sound. . . .

Alexei let his fantasy play out luxuriously.

"Let me get Kira ready to go," he told Toria/Sophia. "I just have to give her my memories.... All my memories will be hers."

Groping around in the dark for his sleeping child, Alexei's fingers brushed the real Sophia's face. He stifled a shiver.

"Go sit on the stairs and wait," Alexei said brusquely. "I want a few minutes alone with my daughter."

As soon as Toria/Sophia was gone, he switched the flashlight back on and hooked up the computer. He was crying while he worked.

And that was the end of my father's memories.

I wanted to believe that he'd cradled and kissed me before handing me over to Toria/Sophia. To Mom. I wanted to believe that he'd swept her into a romantic embrace before sending her off. But of course he wouldn't have, because she wouldn't have understood. I still wasn't sure that I understood. For thirteen years my mother had been the wrong person. And she herself knew the secrets that Rona sought—but even Rona didn't recognize her anymore.

My mother could die never knowing who she really was.

"Kira!" Lynne hissed in my ear. "Kira! We're landing! What's your plan?"

Thirty-Three

I LOOKED AROUND IN CONFUSION, MY MIND STILL back in Crythe more than a dozen years before. The vast, empty field that passed for the Willistown airport lay nearly below us, getting closer with every second. It looked like a foreign landscape to me now—all that openness, all that level ground stretching from horizon to horizon. In less than twenty-four hours I'd grown accustomed to mountains, plunging roads, secrets hiding around every bend.

"You have to tell me your plan," Lynne insisted, "so I know what to do. It's *time*."

I shook my head, unable to speak, unable to explain. Plan? I doubted if even Lynne could have emerged from the sea of memories I was drowning in with a coherent thought, let alone a plan.

Lynne read my blank expression quite accurately.

"Oh no," she whispered. She looked away from me, eyes narrowing. "Uh, Ms. Cummins," she practically shouted toward the front seat. Rona turned only enough to give her a cold stare. Lynne forged on. "Ms. Cummins, I just wanted to make sure—you did take the time difference into account when you were working out all the details of, um, this trip, didn't you? I mean, Ohio is three hours ahead of California, so it's already after seven o'clock here, and I'm pretty sure the bank would be closed by now. . . ."

"The First Bank of Willistown is open until nine P.M. on Thursdays," Rona said icily. "I checked before we left. Don't try to trick me, young lady. You'll regret it."

Lynne gulped and turned pale.

Nobody spoke as we dropped out of the sky and rolled to a stop at the end of a long, vacant slab of concrete. When the pilot cut off the engine, the silence roared in my ears like a giant question. I had the minds of two geniuses linked to my own. Why couldn't I figure out what to do?

"I arranged for a rental car to be delivered here," Rona said. "That must be it over there."

Silently, Lynne and I looked over at a green car parked in an otherwise empty lot. The Willistown airport was mainly a place for weekend hobbyists—

the one or two doctors in town who were rich enough to own a plane. So it was no surprise that the place was deserted on a Thursday evening. But disappointment hit like a rock—I realized that I'd been half hoping we could find somebody here to help.

"Well, come on," Rona said impatiently. Already out of the plane, she was holding the door wide open, waiting for Lynne and me. I awkwardly scrambled out, tripping on the bottom step. "Come on!" Rona repeated.

I turned around, wondering why Lynne was hesitating. But Lynne was on my heels, still linked to me with the rope and cuffs. It was the pilot Rona had yelled at.

He gestured at the instrument panel.

"I take care of plane," he explained.

"Plane? Plane? Forget the plane. We can buy a new one after all this is over. Out!"

In spite of myself, I almost felt sorry for the pilot. An old man should not have to be bossed around by someone half his age.

It was my parents' memories making me think like that, making me think that age required respect.

Shakily, the pilot obeyed Rona and climbed out of the plane. He, Lynne, and I walked a little ahead of Rona, toward the car. She wasn't pointing the gun at any of us now, but she might as well have been.

"Isn't it locked?" Lynne blurted out.

"They said they'd leave the keys in the ignition," Rona practically purred. "You two evidently live in a virtually crime-free town." She laughed, as if she'd made a particularly witty joke.

We piled into the car. Rona made Jacques drive. I kept watching him. If he really was Crythian, shouldn't I recognize him? The only Jacques my parents had known in Crythe had been young and virile. This man was stooped and shaky, gray haired and wrinkled. Half of his face was stiffer than the other side. With my parents' memories, I suddenly understood: He'd had a stroke. Sometime in the past thirteen years, he'd been transformed.

We whipped past cornfields and farmers' houses—places I'd seen before but didn't really know. I could understand now how my parents would have felt about such inattention. How could I *not* have every hillock memorized, every gable of every house ingrained in my mind forever?

Poor Mom, I thought. No wonder she could never fit in in America.

We were on the outskirts of Willistown in no time. Five traffic lights later, we were in the center of town. The pilot parked right in front of the bank. Rona whirled around to face Lynne and me.

"Now," she said to Lynne, "we are leaving you in the car. Keep your head down and stay out of sight. Jacques will have a gun. He will not hesitate to shoot."

She made a big show of producing a new gun from her purse; so she and the pilot each had one. At least one. What if Rona had another two or three firearms stashed somewhere on her?

That thought alone was enough to keep me quiet.

"And you," she said, turning to face me. "I want you to understand. I have a cell phone with me, preprogrammed to call Jacques. If you try anything—anything at all—I'll hit the call button and he will shoot your friend. And then he'll call Crythe and they'll kill your mother. Do you understand?"

Her eyes gleamed maliciously. I hated her, for all my parents' memories. And my own.

Lynne and I exchanged frantic looks.

"But—," I protested weakly. "I want Lynne to go with me. Into the bank."

I should have been steeling myself for that statement ever since we left Crythe, instead of dwelling on the past. I sounded about as authoritative as a gnat.

"Right," Rona said, almost laughing. "They probably have the 'Teen Disappears' signs plastered all over the place in there already. I don't feel like getting arrested for kidnapping now, when I'm so close. And, hey, I didn't kidnap her. Think anyone would believe that?"

"I've been missing too," I said, even more faintly. "Don't you think I'm on those posters too?"

"Oh, but I called in an absence report to your school this morning," Rona said. "They won't be expecting you all week. Do you think I'm stupid?"

No, I thought I was. Rona had everything planned. She'd arranged details I hadn't even thought about. And for the whole plane ride, when I could have been planning, I'd done nothing but wallow in memory, reaching for a father who'd been dead for years, a mother who might as well be. Who probably would be soon because I couldn't help her.

I blinked back tears. This was when I was supposed to be strong, absolutely refusing to go without Lynne. I was supposed to remind Rona about Mom, sacrificing her, and demand, *Do you think I'd do anything to get my mother killed? Why does it matter to you if Lynne goes with us or not?* But I couldn't do it. I couldn't speak the words "mother" and "killed" in the same sentence.

"All right," I said heavily.

I looked once more at Lynne—and shouldn't have. Her face was white with terror.

This is what it feels like to betray someone, I thought. But I already knew that feeling, because of my parents' memories. They'd felt as though they'd betrayed everyone in Crythe.

Wordlessly, I let Rona untie us and unlock the handcuffs. I had rope burns on my leg, and my wrist was sore from where the cuff had rubbed, but I still wanted to protest, *No! Don't separate us!*

I kept silent. I climbed out of the car and stood beside Rona on the familiar sidewalk. A few cars drove by, but I didn't see anyone I knew—certainly not anyone I knew well enough to signal secretly: *Call the police! I'm in danger! Lynne's in that car! Mom's being held hostage in California!*

What kind of signal did I think could convey all that? And what did I expect anyone to do?

We climbed the stone steps. I tried to tell myself that Lynne was safer with the pilot than she would have been with me and Rona. He didn't seem to have Rona's killer instinct.

But he didn't seem to have much desire to disobey Rona, either.

Rona held the door open for me.

"Now, act normal," she hissed as we stepped onto the tile floor.

"Normal." What did that word mean, again?

I glanced around, trying not to look as petrified as I felt. A woman sitting at a desk asked, "May I help you?"

I thought maybe the woman was Carl Dotson's mom. He was in the same grade as me at school, and I could remember his mother coming in to help with the holiday parties when we were in elementary school. She'd made heart cookies for Valentine's Day, pumpkin cookies at Halloween.

No matter what Crythians believed, my memories didn't do me any good. Mrs. Dotson couldn't help me either.

"My niece here needs to get into her safe-deposit box," Rona said smoothly, her voice containing just enough boredom to make it sound like *she* didn't much care about that box, but it was something *I* wanted, and she was the type of kindly aunt who would indulge her niece's wishes.

"Of course," Mrs. Dotson said. "Have a seat, and I'll pull your card. What's the number on that box?"

I dug the key from my pocket and read off the number in a mechanical voice: "Twenty. Seven."

"Okay. I'll be right back," Mrs. Dotson said. She walked back behind the counter where all the tellers stood. Neither Rona nor I sank into the leather chairs by Mrs. Dotson's desk. Rona stood at rigid attention, her cell phone clutched very conspicuously in her right hand. My knees trembled, and I felt faint. In seconds Mrs. Dotson was bound to come back and say that number 27 was Mom's safe-deposit box, not mine. And then Rona would know the truth, and she'd press the button on her phone, and Lynne would be dead. And so would Mom.

I had to stop that from happening. But how?

I swayed a little, and the back of my legs brushed Mrs. Dotson's desk. That gave me an idea. It was a pretty feeble one, but at that point, I was willing to try anything. I groped behind me, hoping Mrs. Dotson was the type to use a letter opener. Then before Mrs. Dotson came back, I could stab at Rona before she had a chance to call the pilot out in the car with Lynne. With a letter opener, I could save us all.

My hand closed on something behind me. A pen. Was a pen a good enough weapon? I didn't think so, but I kept it in my hand anyway. You know you're desperate when your best hope is a twenty-nine-cent Bic.

Mrs. Dotson was walking back to us now. Rona glanced my way and deliberately placed her finger just above one of the cell phone's buttons. I got the message.

"Okay, Kira," Mrs. Dotson said. "Right this way."

I let out a deep breath, realizing for the first

time that I'd been holding it ever since she walked away. But relief was a ridiculous emotion. This was only a reprieve. As soon as Rona discovered that there was nothing she wanted in the safe-deposit box, Lynne and Mom were dead.

Somehow I managed to propel myself forward, following Mrs. Dotson. Rona was right behind me. I could hear her heels clicking on the tile. Each step sounded like a gunshot. Then, just as we reached the bank vault, Mrs. Dotson turned around.

"Oh, I'm sorry, ma'am," she said to Rona. "I'm afraid you'll have to wait for your niece over there. It's bank policy that only boxholders themselves are allowed into the vault."

Rona frowned. I could tell she hadn't anticipated this. She squinted suspiciously at Mrs. Dotson. Then she regained her composure.

"Oh, of course. I can understand that for adults. But my niece here is a minor, and—"

"And minors are certainly entitled to rights too, don't you think?" Mrs. Dotson said sweetly. The smile on her face very clearly said, *I'm going to be pleasant about this, but don't think that means I'm giving in.*

Rona looked from Mrs. Dotson to me, considering. Finally, she said loudly, "My niece has no secrets from me, do you, Kira?"

She wanted me to say, *Oh, no, Auntie. Come along. I want you with me. I insist.* Did I have to? If I didn't take her into the vault with me, would she call the pilot and order Lynne's death? And Mom's?

Mrs. Dotson saved me from having to decide.

"How nice for the two of you," she said to Rona. Her voice might as well have been dripping honey. "I didn't mean to imply otherwise. But rules are rules, and I've learned that the only way for me to keep my job is to follow them. I'm sorry. Now, if you would . . . ?" She gestured toward the chairs by her desk. I loved Mrs. Dotson suddenly. I could see Rona relenting.

"Well, I wouldn't want to ask you to bend any rules on my behalf, no matter how trifling those rules might seem," she said. "All right, Kira. I'll be waiting right here when you come out." Somehow she made those words sound warm and support-ive, like a loving aunt promising to be there when her niece needed her. But I could hear the threat behind the words. She held her phone up. "If you're in there a long time, maybe I'll even take care of some business calls."

I felt the color draining from my face.

"I—I'm sure this won't take that long," I stam-mered.

Rona sat down—not in the chairs Mrs. Dotson had pointed to, but right behind us, as close to the vault as she could possibly get. Mrs. Dotson watched her for a second, then led me on into the vault.

Thirty-Four

I'D BEEN IN THIS VAULT ONCE BEFORE, ON SOME GRADE school field trip. I can remember being impressed by the thick walls, the way you could see the stone between the metal on either side of the door. The bank official who led the tour had stressed how safe everything was in the vault—from fire, thieves, tornadoes, floods—"from all the dangers of the world," he'd said.

I didn't feel safe in there now. All I could think about was how those thick walls prevented me from seeing what Rona was doing. I had no way of knowing if she was right now raising the phone toward her mouth, giving the orders I would do anything to prevent.

Not that I could think of anything to do.

Heart pounding, I trudged behind Mrs. Dotson. She led me toward the farthest end of the vault. The numbers, I saw with surprise, were in the fifties and getting larger, not smaller. Finally, in the very back corner of the vault, she whirled around.

"All right, Kira," she whispered. "What is going on?"

"You— You know who I am?" I whispered back.

"Well, based on the card I pulled, I should be looking at Sophia Landon right now, not Kira. But, good grief, of course I know you. Carl had a crush on you all through seventh grade. All we heard for a whole year was, 'Kira this' and 'Kira that.'"

In spite of myself, I blushed.

"And, anyhow," Mrs. Dotson continued, "that's all anybody's been talking about today—where you and your mom disappeared to, and whether or not you took Lynne Robertson with you."

My knees went weak with relief. Everything was going to be all right. Why did I think I had to solve my problems by myself? I'd just spill the whole story to Mrs. Dotson, and she'd take care of Mom, Lynne, and me.

"Lynne Robertson is sitting in a car out front, with a man pointing a gun at her," I said. "And Mom's being held hostage in California. And that woman who came into the bank with me—"

"Is no aunt of yours," Mrs. Dotson finished for me. "That's all I needed to know." She reached for a button on the wall. I watched her as though the scene were in slow motion: her arm extending, her finger pointing, her jacket sleeve sliding back on her wrist. . . .

"What are you doing?" I asked, dazed.

"I'm calling the police. This is our alarm system."

"No, wait," I said, suddenly jolted out of my daze. How could I have thought, even for a second, that this could be easy? "Don't call the police. If they try to arrest Rona—that woman—she'll signal to the guy in the car to kill Lynne. And he'll signal the people in California to kill Mom."

Mrs. Dotson's finger hovered over the button.

"The alarm doesn't sound inside the bank," she said. "That woman will never know what we're doing. And the police can arrest the man in the car first," she said, sounding as matter-of-fact as she had years ago, reminding second graders that they were allowed only one cup of Halloween punch.

I stared at Mrs. Dotson's finger poised beside the button, and I experienced something like double vision: I could very clearly see another woman's finger about to dial a phone, I could picture an old man's finger on a trigger. I remembered Lynne's look of stark terror. And I remembered Willistown's police chief, a bumbling man whose greatest talent was playing Santa Claus every year on the courthouse lawn. I couldn't imagine him managing to disarm the pilot before the pilot shot Lynne. Maybe I'd have had confidence in him if I hadn't had my parents' memories in my mind—I could remember seeing people shot. Through them, I'd witnessed plenty of murders.

I shook my head stubbornly.

"No, Mrs. Dotson. Please. You don't understand. It's very complicated. I don't have time to explain, but the police can't help right now."

Mrs. Dotson looked at me questioningly, but she moved her arm back from the wall.

"All right," she said briskly. "What do you want me to do? What's your plan?"

It was the same question Lynne had asked me, back on the plane. Just that word, "plan," practically sent me into the same kind of hysterical laughter Lynne had erupted into at the thought of airplane peanuts. *Plan, plan, everyone wants a plan. And all I've managed to do is grab a cheap ink pen.* Feebly, I raised my hand toward Mrs. Dotson, as if the pen itself could explain all my inadequacies. Puzzled, Mrs. Dotson peered at the Bic balanced in my palm. I stared at it too. After a few seconds I opened my eyes wider, really seeing it for the first time.

It was just a cheap ink pen. But that was exactly what I needed right now.

I had a plan.

Thirty-Five

"P-P-PAPER," I SPUTTERED AT MRS. DOTSON. "I NEED paper. But she can't see you leaving the vault to go get it."

Mrs. Dotson patted her pockets and came up with one of those half-size pads that businesses give away all the time. It said FIRST BANK OF WILLIS-TOWN at the top of every sheet.

"No," I objected. "It has to look like something my father might have written on thirteen or fourteen years ago in California."

Mrs. Dotson frowned and looked down at the key ring she carried in her hand.

"Let's see what your mom keeps in her safe-deposit box," she said.

We walked back toward the front of the vault, to box number 27.

"Your father, you say?" Mrs. Dotson muttered curiously. "How's he figure in all of this?"

I shook my head impatiently. Mrs. Dotson got the hint and focused on opening the box.

"Your mom has always had our biggest box size," Mrs. Dotson said. "Everyone at the bank always wondered why—not that any of us ever looked," she added virtuously.

She discreetly stepped back while I slid the box out and opened the lid. There, on top of the pile, were the important papers I'd searched our entire apartment for only two days ago: my birth certificate, my parents' citizenship papers, their marriage license. I didn't have time for those documents right now; and, anyhow, through my parents' memories, I knew all of them by heart already. I whipped through the papers, just praying for a blank sheet. There wasn't one. I reached the bottom of the stack, uncovering a shoe box underneath.

I knew what was in the shoe box, so I ignored it for now. I pulled out the blank, white envelope from my parents' marriage license and began scrawling on it in my best imitation of my father's writing. It was weird—I could *remember* how to form the letters the way he had, but my hand balked at writing the unfamiliar script.

"Kira? What are you doing?" Mrs. Dotson asked behind me. "Are you— Is that *Russian* you're writing?"

"Yep," I said grimly, and kept writing. I threw in a diagram or two for good measure, the way I did on geometry tests when I wasn't sure of my answer and I hoped I could distract the teacher.

I couldn't believe how stupid I'd been before. I felt like Dorothy in *The Wizard of Oz*, wandering around all over the place searching for a way to get back home, when the whole time she'd been wearing the ruby slippers that could take her there. The whole time I'd been worrying about what Rona would do when I emerged from the vault empty-handed, I'd had the very information she wanted tucked away in my mind.

I just wasn't going to give her quite what she expected.

I lowered my pen and reread what I'd written. Could I fool Rona? Because of my parents' memories, I knew the exact limits of her computer abilities. But what if she'd learned a lot in thirteen years?

I had to take my chances.

I eased the shoe box out from under the papers and tucked it under my arm.

"I'm done, Mrs. Dotson," I said. "Thanks for everything. If you don't hear from me first, could you call the police and tell them to come and arrest a pair of kidnappers at my house at"—I did some mental math—"eleven o'clock tonight?"

Mrs. Dotson looked at me doubtfully.

"Are you *sure* you don't want me to call the police right now?" she said. "This isn't some kids' game. You don't want to fool around with people with guns."

"I know," I said grimly. "But I'm trying to save my mother's life."

I could tell that Mrs. Dotson believed me. I looked at her, an ordinary woman in an unfash-ionable navy blue jacket, and I realized that she was showing an incredible amount of faith in me. It seemed like I really ought to say something else, to make her understand how much I appreciated that.

"Mrs. Dotson?" I said. "I always thought you made the world's best pumpkin cookies."

Then I walked out of the vault toward Rona.

Thirty-Six

RONA JERKED TO ATTENTION AS SOON AS I WALKED out, then I could see her reminding herself to act casual. I'm sure I was the only one in the bank who saw her eyes narrow, her lip curl.

"What's in the box?" she asked as soon as I got close enough that she could talk to me without being overheard.

"Computer disks," I said, doing my best to match her fake nonchalance. "I thought they might be important. Here are my father's notes." I handed her the envelope I'd just covered in Cyrillic letters.

Rona's jaw dropped. "It's in Russian," she said. Even she wasn't able to hide the dismay in her voice.

I shrugged, pretending not to understand why this bothered her.

"That's where he was from," I said.

"No, he was from Crythe," she hissed at me.

"Well, he was educated in Russia," I said. "Anyhow, you have what you want now. Call Crythe and tell them to let my mother go. And tell Jacques not to shoot Lynne."

"How do I know if I have what I want or not?" Rona demanded. She was still speaking quietly, but her voice was packed with fury, an explosion waiting to happen. "I can't read Russian."

It took every shred of acting ability I had not to let out a deep sigh of relief.

"Lynne can," I volunteered. "She's been taking Russian since sixth grade."

This was my biggest gamble. The high school in Willistown doesn't offer Russian—the middle school doesn't offer any foreign languages at all. And even Lynne wasn't brilliant enough to pick it up on her own. But I had to make Lynne seem essential to Rona, at least for another hour or two.

Rona forced her lips into one long, narrow, bitter line. She was deciding.

"Let's go see how good she is at translations," she said finally.

We walked out of the bank together. Out of the corner of my eye, I could see Rona shaking her head at the pilot as we walked down the steps. As soon as we got to the car, she whipped open the door and said to the pilot, in Crythian, "Don't kill her."

So I had been right, and they'd been planning to kill Lynne no matter what, as soon as Rona got what she wanted. My body wanted to go limp at this revelation, to slide down into a terrified heap right there on the sidewalk. But some combination of my parents' grit and my own dumb hope and loyalty kept me walking.

I circled around Rona and slid into the backseat with Lynne while Rona climbed into the front. I immediately leaned over and whispered in Lynne's ear.

"I told Rona that you know Russian," I said quickly. "You have a terrible accent, so you sound awful when you speak it, but you can read it pretty well. When she gives you a document to translate, say she has to have the computer first. Say it's really technical and it only makes sense if she's got the special computer in front of her."

I was done talking and had backed away from Lynne before Rona was completely settled in the front. Lynne looked totally baffled, but she might have looked like that anyway, wondering what had happened in the bank. Rona turned around and gave the two of us a warning look.

"We'll proceed to the next phase of my plan," Rona said. "There's been a little complication. Neither of you is safe yet. Sophia isn't either. So get down!"

She added that last part because a car was driving past. Lynne and I both immediately lurched inward, almost clunking heads.

"But I *don't* know Russian!" Lynne protested quietly. Both of us had our cheeks pressed against the vinyl seats, our hair covering our faces.

"You'll have to pretend," I said grimly.

"Tell me what to say!" Lynne pleaded.

"Shh," I said.

In the front Rona was giving Jacques directions in Crythian. Their voices were muffled and, I realized, Rona's accent was bad. But I could mostly follow their conversation.

"We'll go to Sophia's apartment," Rona said. "We can hide there and get the girl to translate."

"And then you'll help me?" Jacques said quietly.

"Of course," Rona said impatiently. "I'll fix you right up. After you carry through on your end of the bargain."

I didn't want to think about whatever it was that Jacques had agreed to do. I already had enough suspicions. As Jacques pulled away from the curb I started quickly telling Lynne exactly what to say about my father's forged notes.

"How am I supposed to remember all that?" Lynne protested.

"Well, it'd be natural if you stumbled some," I said. "Just remember to ask for the computer first."

Lynne was quiet for a minute. Then she said, "I feel like the girl in 'Rumpelstiltskin.'"

"Huh?" I said.

"You know, the one whose dad said she could spin straw into gold."

I had to grin behind my curtain of hair. Trust Lynne—even under threat of death, she was coming up with the kinds of analogies and allusions teachers loved.

Then my grin faded. Threat of death. Lynne knew. She knew the girl in the fairy tale would have been killed if she hadn't produced the gold, and she knew she was going to be killed if she couldn't fake knowing Russian.

"What if they figure out that the paper doesn't really say what I'm telling them?" Lynne asked.

"Oh, but it does," I said. "I know. I wrote it."

Lynne raised her face from the seat just enough to peer curiously at me.

"Since when do you know Russian?" she asked.

"Since you hypnotized me on the plane," I said.

We stopped talking while Jacques waited at a traffic light. As soon as the car accelerated again and the engine was loud enough to cover the sound of our whispers, Lynne said, "You can't do this to me! You've got to explain how I—"

But Jacques was pulling into our gravel driveway just then. Lynne bit off her question, clamped her mouth shut. I turned my head slightly so I could see the view out the window: familiar willow branches, our neighbor's cream-colored siding.

I had never been so conscious before of how close our house was to the house next door. Mrs. Dotson had said everyone in town was talking about Mom and me disappearing—what if one of the neighbors heard the car and came to welcome us home or (more likely) to try to find out where we'd been? Rona was not exactly in a neighborly mood. The best we could hope for was that she'd take more hostages, instead of shooting.

Wanting to protect all my neighbors in Willistown, I understood better than ever how my parents had felt about their fellow Crythians.

"Okay. Everybody out," Rona ordered us. "Up the stairs quickly. Kira, do you have the key?"

Miraculously, I still did. I let us all in. I steeled myself against remembering how naive I'd been, leaving home with Rona only the night before. The phone still sat askew on the window ledge, right where I'd left it when I'd been too stupid to call the police.

But if I had called the police the night before, what would have happened to Mom?

Rona saw me eyeing the phone. She pulled the jack out of the wall.

"Don't get any ideas," she warned me.

We sat on the living-room floor, away from all the windows. Rona thrust the envelope at Lynne.

"Kira says you can read Russian. Tell me what this says," she demanded.

Lynne squinted at the envelope.

"The writing's really bad," she muttered. She sounded like she was really offended, not just stalling for time. "But here goes. First, you have to have the special computer—"

Rona swore.

"Those were supposed to be the directions for building the special computer!" she yelled. "Aren't there notes about that?"

Lynne looked up, slightly annoyed, a scholar interrupted in her studies. I was terrified that Lynne was going to carry this act a little too far.

"Mom has a special computer," I said quickly.

"Huh?" Lynne said, too fast. She was startled into an honest reaction.

"Well, I don't know if it's the right one. I've seen it only once or twice. She never let me use it. She said it was a reminder of my father—this was when I thought she was my real mother, you know. . . . I thought it was just a sentimental thing."

"Where's the blasted computer?" Rona exploded.

I tilted my head to the side. This was my

imitation of a not-very-bright kid doing her best to think. Lynne glared. She probably thought *I* was overacting.

"Out in the car?" I hazarded.

I really wasn't sure. I just remembered the strange look on Mom's face, back in Crythe, when she was talking about me driving the car to Lynne's. I said before that claiming that Lynne knew Russian was my biggest gamble, but this was actually bigger.

Probably I'd decide that at every step of my plan. The whole thing was touch and go.

I didn't like to think about that.

"Show me," Rona said. She was so tense, she barely moved her lips.

We left Lynne with Jacques again, and I led Rona down to the old garage behind the house.

As soon as I saw the car, I was flooded with memories. My parents had bought this car soon after they came to the United States; they'd used it every day for years to drive between Crythe and their computer jobs. Between worlds. They'd worked out a lot of their plans sitting in those two front seats.

I ached, remembering a time before I was even born.

I also remembered my father hiding the car down the hill from Crythe, the night Mom and I escaped. He'd stashed one thing in the trunk: the shoe box I'd retrieved from Mom's safe-deposit box. The computer disks inside it contained the copied memories of every single person in Crythe.

I knew that when my father had copied his own memories into my mind, he fully intended to send Mom away with both the laptop computer and me. I was certain he wouldn't have changed his mind. And I was certain that Mom would never have thrown the computer away. I'd searched the apartment, and it wasn't there. So it had to still be in the car. Didn't it?

"Where is it?" Rona asked suspiciously.

She had her gun out again. I suddenly realized that she thought I had a weapon hidden out here.

Why hadn't I thought to hide a weapon out here, oh, say, a night or two ago?

But I needed Rona alive, to tell the Crythians not to kill Mom.

I unlocked the car door, and it swung open with a rusty creak. The seats were empty. I felt around on the floor. Nothing. I opened the trunk. Still nothing. I looked under the mat where the spare tire should have been. Nothing again. I went back to the front of the car and peeked in the glove compartment, even though it was too small to hold even a laptop. All I found there was another key to our apartment.

"Well?" Rona snarled.

I snatched up the key, my fingers closing around the jagged edge. Then a funny thing happened. I could tell without looking that the indentations on this key were different from the ones on my apartment key. I never would have said it was possible to memorize the feel of grooves on a key, but I had.

Or my parents' minds had.

It was scary having my parents' minds inside my own. Where did they leave off and I begin?

I didn't have time for philosophical questions. I held up the key and said, with much more confidence than I actually felt, "Mom hid the computer on the third floor of our house. This is the key to the storage area up there."

"I thought you said the computer was here in the car," Rona growled.

"I didn't know Mom moved it," I argued. "Do you think I can read her mind?"

"What if she moved it more than once? How can you tell that's the right key? Why didn't Sophia leave a nice little label, 'If you're looking for the special computer, use this'?" Rona demanded mockingly.

I shrugged and didn't answer. But I dared to turn around and walk out of the garage, hoping that Rona would follow me. I wasn't sure that she had until I was halfway up the back stairs and I heard her footsteps behind me.

"It had better be there, that's all I can say," Rona hissed as we reached the third-floor door.

I put the key in the lock and turned. The door squeaked open. All the windows on the third floor were covered, so the only light came from behind us. It took my eyes a few minutes to adjust to the dimness. At first I thought the room in front of us was totally vacant, nothing but floor and ceiling and walls. Then I saw it, off to the side, the only object my mother had seen fit to put into storage: the computer.

Thirty-Seven

RONA POUNCED ON THE COMPUTER BEFORE I HAD A
chance to move.

"Do you know how long I've been looking for
this?" she chortled. She hugged the computer to her
chest almost tenderly, as if it were a beloved child.

"I thought you just wanted the directions for
making it," I said uneasily.

"Oh, I can figure that out, if I have the model,"
she said carelessly. "Come on. I want to try it out."

"On Jacques?" I said tentatively. For a minute I
was afraid that Rona would be magnanimous,
helping Jacques instead of herself. I should have
known Rona better than that.

"Jacques?" she repeated incredulously. "Of
course not. On me!"

We went back down the stairs to our apartment, where Jacques and Lynne were staring at
each other, the gun balanced on his knee.

"Okay!" Rona announced gleefully. "Let's try this baby out. What's the first step?"

Lynne peered down at the Cyrillic writing.

"Um, you need Sophia's fingerprint to get into the system. Like a password," Lynne said.

"What!" Rona exploded. "You're lying!"

Lynne held up her hands helplessly.

"I'm just reading what it says," she said innocently.

Rona ripped the envelope out of Lynne's hand. I congratulated myself on having remembered to draw a finger, complete with realistic whorls, near the computer. I'd written *Sophia* above it, just to make sure.

Rona lowered the page and glared at me.

"Did you know about this?" she demanded.

"What do you mean?" I asked. "I never even heard of Crythe until yesterday. How could I have known anything?" I tried to keep a straight face, as innocent as apple pie.

Maybe I succeeded, because Rona looked back at the paper.

"Sophia!" she said, like a curse. "She knew!"

My heart dropped. I hadn't anticipated this. Rona was angrier than ever at my mom, and it was all my fault. Why hadn't I thought of a different plan?

"Wow, Kira," Lynne said, looking over Rona's shoulder at the diagram. "Your father was way ahead of his time. He wrote this thirteen years ago, right? Other scientists are just now starting to do fingerprint IDs."

I groaned inwardly. Lynne and her big mouth. Rona was looking at me suspiciously again.

"How fast can you have the plane ready to go back to Crythe?" she asked Jacques in Crythian.

"Now?" Jacques said. He looked thoroughly exhausted. "It'd take quite a while. I'd have to refuel, check my systems. . . ."

Rona glanced at her watch and grimaced. I forced myself to keep my face blank, but I felt like grimacing too. How could Rona want to go back to Crythe? I'd been banking on her bringing Mom here. Jacques had just flown from Crythe, after flying there only last night. Weren't there rules about pilots resting between long flights?

Of course, how could I expect Rona to follow any rules?

"Okay. Here's what we do," Rona finally said to Jacques, still speaking Crythian. "We get the rest of the document translated, then we kill both girls, hide their bodies, and go back to Crythe."

My knees went weak, but I had to pretend I didn't understand. I swayed only slightly. *Think, think, think,* I commanded myself.

"What if Sophia won't cooperate?" Jacques asked.

"All we need is her fingerprint," Rona said impatiently. "She doesn't even have to be alive for us to get that."

That sent me over the edge. I jumped at Rona, yanked the computer from her arms, and backed away, holding the computer high over my head. I was fast. By the time Rona had her gun out and pointed at me, I was halfway across the room, standing in front of Lynne like a shield.

"If you squeeze that trigger," I said, "I'll drop the computer. You can kill me, but it won't do you any good."

I was surprised that my voice came out sounding strong and sure, like Clint Eastwood or Bruce Willis or any of those other hotshot movie stars who probably would have trembled if a gun were pointed at them in real life. I was trembling myself, but it evidently didn't affect my voice box.

"Now," I said quickly, before I could realize how scared I really was, "you call Crythe and make arrangements for Mom to be flown here. Because I am holding this computer hostage. You are not getting it back until my mother walks through that door."

"Kira," Lynne whispered behind me, "what are you doing? She's got a *gun*."

"And I've got the computer. And you've got the

directions," I said, without turning around. "She won't hurt us."

I held the computer straight up. If I dropped it, it would fall six feet. Was that enough to destroy a laptop computer? I had to convince Rona that it was.

"If you shoot me and I drop this, you'll never learn my parents' secrets," I said, doing my best to sound cool and logical. "Think how long you've been waiting. Think how much of your life you would have wasted on this. On nothing. A bunch of scrambled circuitry you could never put back together. Why not play it safe, do what I say?"

Rona still had her gun pointed at me, but I could tell she was wavering. I remembered my father trying to reason with her when she'd found out about his experiments. He'd been naive, trusting her, expecting her to understand that the research he did was just for Crythians, because Crythians were different from other people. He expected a woman who saw herself as alone in the world, with no obligation to anyone, to understand his sense of obligation to an entire village.

She hadn't understood. And he hadn't understood her.

But I'd been raised as an American. I understood greed better than my parents had. I knew that Rona saw money when she looked at the computer, nothing else. No moral issues, no ethical dilemmas, no humanitarian concerns. I knew Rona was imagining a fortune crashing to the floor, evaporating on the spot.

"Jacques," she finally said, "can you find one of your old flying buddies to bring Sophia here?"

"I—I guess so," he stammered. "You want Howard? George? Or—"

"I don't care who it is!" Rona snapped.

"Call Crythe," I commanded. "Tell them not to kill Mom. Tell them to let Mom go."

Rona glared at me. But slowly, very slowly, she pulled her cell phone out again and began dialing.

Thirty-Eight

GRABBING THE COMPUTER HAD SEEMED LIKE A brilliant idea during the half second I'd had to think about it before I leaped at Rona. Somehow I'd managed not to dwell on how hard it would be to hold the computer up in the air, threateningly, for hours.

After just ten minutes my arms were aching. If I didn't concentrate on commanding my muscles, *Stay up, stay up, stay up,* I'd find myself lowering the computer down, down, down—and then, horrified, I'd snap it back up again.

Rona didn't seem to be having any problem at all keeping her gun aimed steadily at my head. She stared just as steadily.

"How did you get so smart all of a sudden?" she asked abruptly, when we'd been glaring at each other in silence for what felt like an eternity. "How did you know that I wasn't planning to bring Sophia here anyway before you grabbed the computer?"

My arms felt weaker than ever.

"I—I guessed," I stammered.

"Why is it so important to you to stay here?" she asked.

I couldn't say, *Because I was afraid you'd kill us before you returned to Crythe.* I couldn't say, *Because I was afraid you'd kill Mom if I didn't bargain for her life.* My mind flickered on a detail I'd half forgotten: the possibility that the police would come and rescue us at eleven o'clock, if Mrs. Dotson had done what I'd asked her to. Mom would still be in the airplane then. Would she be safe?

I had to hope so. But I couldn't let Rona see that I had any hopes at all.

"Crythe scared me," I said flatly. "I didn't like it there."

Rona threw back her head and laughed uproariously.

"A bunch of half-wits living in the past?" she asked contemptuously. "The terrified remnants of a failed experiment? Crythe is *nothing.* Right, Jacques?"

"Huh?" Jacques was practically asleep, huddled against the wall behind her.

"Forget it, Jacques," Rona said in disgust. We all watched as Jacques's eyelids drooped again.

"When this is over, I'll be able to hire the best and brightest again," Rona said. "Like your parents. Did you know that they used to work for me?"

I did, but I had to pretend that I didn't.

"Doing what?" I asked.

"Oh, they were my ringers. R and D. Research and Development. I had this little computer company, see, that was up against the big guys. And your parents developed the greatest system, something that would make Bill Gates look like a two-bit idiot. But they had funny ideas about who owned their inventions." She looked at me sadly. "This is really just about patent rights, intellectual property . . . business matters."

Liar! I wanted to shout. My parents had done their Crythe research on their own time, with their own equipment. Rona had no right to their work. Their mistake was in telling her anything. But I couldn't defend my parents without giving away everything.

"You're supposed to settle those problems in court, not with guns," Lynne said boldly behind me. I turned around to give her a quick grin of gratitude.

"Oh, I forgot. They teach idealism in school nowadays." Rona chuckled. "You'll learn. The way the real world works—sometimes you just have to take what belongs to you."

I knew I could trust Lynne to debate that. I was glad we'd managed to distract Rona from trying to figure me out. But my arms were trembling from holding the computer aloft for so long. This wasn't going to work.

"Stand up, Lynne," I said quietly while Rona was still chuckling.

Lynne scrambled up instantly. Rona stopped laughing and tightened her grip on the gun.

"I have to go to the bathroom," I announced. "Lynne's going to hold the computer now."

I didn't give Rona time to object. It was only a second before Lynne had the computer held high over her own head, her eyes locked on Rona's.

Could we do this for the next several hours—pass the computer back and forth whenever we got tired?

No.

I bent my head toward Lynne's ear, pretending I was just reaching out to steady the computer.

"Jump into the bathroom the same time as me and we'll lock the door," I whispered.

Lynne flashed me a startled look that Rona had to have noticed. I watched the suspicion play over Rona's face as Lynne and I inched backward, in unison, toward the bathroom.

"She's protecting me," I told Rona. "We're just making sure you don't shoot either one of us."

"I could kill you both with one shot," she countered. "Stop right there!"

We were on the threshold to the bathroom. I responded by jerking Lynne around behind me, slamming the door, and flattening myself against the wall, all in one smooth move. Lynne stumbled and sprawled across the length of the floor.

"I said to stop!" Rona screamed.

I turned the lock on the door. Seconds later a bullet whistled through the middle panel of the door.

Lynne rolled over and dove into the bathtub. I figured she knew what she was doing. I jumped after her.

"Is this tub porcelain or ceramic?" Lynne whispered.

"I don't know—it's old, that's all," I said, irked that she could ask such a stupid question when all I wanted to do was listen for the next bullet.

"But will it protect us, or should we hide behind the toilet?"

"I don't want to risk getting shot while I'm switching places," I replied.

The bathtub did seem safe. It was off to the side, not in the direct line of fire if Rona shot at the door again. I never thought I'd be looking at anything with claw feet as a safe haven.

"That didn't hit you, did it?" Lynne asked.

I hadn't even thought to check. I looked down. All my skin cells seemed to be connected to one another, unpunctured.

"No. What about you?"

"I'm fine. And the computer—" She held it up, and both of us stared.

Rona's bullet had gone right through the center of the computer.

Thirty-Nine

MY FIRST REACTION WAS UTTERLY RIDICULOUS. MY eyes filled with tears, and I wanted to whimper, *Papa. Mama.*

That computer *had* been my parents' most impressive invention, and now it was destroyed. For a second I felt the surge of nostalgia that I'd claimed Mom had felt for this computer.

Lynne didn't have the same kind of emotional connection to waylay her.

"Hey, hey!" she shouted out to Rona. "Don't shoot again. I know you don't care about us, but you might hit the computer! Just leave us alone, and we'll come out as soon as we hear Sophia's voice."

"You'll climb out the window," Rona said.

"From the second floor? We'd be killed. Send Jacques out to watch for us if you're so worried."

"You might as well come out of there. I'm going to pick the lock," Rona said.

"Can she do that?" Lynne whispered frantically to me.

Silently, I shook my head.

"I don't think so," I said. One advantage of living in such an old house was that all the locks on the doors really worked. At Lynne's house all we needed was a bent bobby pin and we could break into any room in the house. "And there's not a key anywhere. One time we locked ourselves out, and we had to borrow Mrs. Steele's ladder and break the window to get in."

"What if Rona does something like that?" Lynne asked, panicked.

"She'd attract too much attention. Wouldn't she?" I asked.

Outside the bathroom, Rona yelled again: "Maybe I'll take the door off the hinges."

"Oh no," I moaned. "I'm so stupid."

But Lynne didn't look worried.

"The hinges are on this side!" she yelled back to Rona. Then she whispered to me, "Didn't you know that when you decided to lock us in here?"

"Oh, sure," I muttered. "Of course." But my heart pounded because I *hadn't* thought about hinges. Even my parents had never had to lock themselves in a bathroom to protect themselves from a gunslinging maniac.

"Don't feel bad," Lynne said, seeing right through me. "I probably shouldn't have told her where the hinges were. Then she would have wasted time looking for something to take the door off. . . ."

I ignored Lynne's apology.

"What else could go wrong?" I asked desperately.

"Nothing, unless she tries to shoot off the lock," Lynne whispered back. That was something else I hadn't thought of. Lynne saw from my expression that she had to take charge.

"Just leave us alone," she shouted out at Rona. "It's not worth the risk for you to do anything else. If you try to get us out of here, we'll throw the computer out the window and we'll flush the notes down the toilet. Got it?"

Rona didn't answer.

Lynne and I listened, our hearts beating wildly. No more threats, no more gunshots, no tugs at the doorknob.

"Maybe Rona and Jacques left," Lynne finally whispered.

"No," I said. "They're just waiting."

"So what are we going to do?" Lynne asked. "When your mom gets here, I mean.

What are we going to do about the computer?"

"We'd better start praying," I said glumly. "It's our only hope."

That's when we heard the tapping at the window.

Forty

IF THE SOUND HAD BEEN ANY LOUDER, I WOULD HAVE panicked, convinced that Rona or Jacques was going to break the window and that we had only a few minutes before Rona would discover the destroyed computer and kill us both. But the tapping was so faint, I wasn't sure I could trust my own ears.

"Shhh," I whispered to Lynne.

I stood up and crept over to the window. This was the only room in our apartment that had good blinds. I was lucky that they were pulled down. I slowly moved them away from the window, just enough to peek out.

A man's face stared back at me.

"I'm Officer Lanur, miss," he said through the glass. "Are you okay?"

Did he mean apart from having been kidnapped? Apart from practically having a heart attack from the shock of seeing a face at a second-story window?

He was motioning for me to raise the window. I unlatched it and opened it just a crack. I still had the notion I shouldn't do anything I couldn't hide quickly if Rona stormed into the bathroom.

"Did that shot hit either you or your friend?" the man asked.

Mutely, I shook my head.

"Then let's get you out of there," he said.

I stared at him as stupidly as if he'd suggested sprouting wings and flying.

"Unless you *like* being locked in a bathroom and getting shot at," the man said.

I pulled the blinds back farther so I could see him better. He was clinging to a rope hanging down from the roof.

"They're going to see you," I whispered. "I just told her to send the guy out to look. She was worried we'd climb out the window."

I'm not sure how much sense that made. Officer Lanur didn't seem the least bit concerned.

"Your two kidnappers are in the kitchen right now, having a snack," he answered. "Don't worry. We're watching. We set up a stakeout, oh, ten, fifteen minutes ago. We don't like innocent teenagers hanging out with trigger-happy freaks, so we thought we'd rescue you before we did anything else."

Mrs. Dotson, I thought. She didn't wait until eleven to call the police.

She had saved my life.

I decided I should think better of the Willistown police, too, since they'd been able to spy on us all along without anyone noticing.

"What's going on?" Lynne whispered behind me. She joined me at the window and then jumped back in surprise at the sight of an unfamiliar face.

"It's the police," I hissed. "They found us!"

"Pleased to meet you," Officer Lanur said to Lynne. "How about if we continue this conversation on the ground, *after* I get you out of there? I'm getting a little tired of impersonating a spider."

Beside me, Lynne was beaming. I hadn't seen her look so happy since the school officials agreed to let her do an independent study on binary numbers.

"But my mom—," I started to protest.

"You tell us exactly where they're holding her, and we can get her, too," Officer Lanur said. "But let's get you two to safety first."

I was still working that one out—did I deserve to be safe when Mom wasn't yet? But I knew I wanted Lynne out of danger. She was already pushing up the window, palms firmly hoisting at the bottom. The window surged up three inches, then ground to a halt. She bent down, shoved her right shoulder under the window, and pushed. The window didn't budge.

"Why—won't—this—open?" Lynne grunted.

It's funny how, if you're terrified enough, you can forget something you've known all your life.

"That's as far as this window ever opens," I said dully. "Remember?"

Lynne looked crushed and stopped pushing. I could tell she knew what I was talking about. But Officer Lanur still looked puzzled, so I had to enlighten him.

"It's designed that way. One of the kids of the original owner fell out a window and was killed, so the father made it so none of the second- or third-floor windows in the house could open more than four or five inches. When Mrs. Steele bought this house, she had all the other windows replaced. But she didn't bother changing the windows in the bathroom."

I was babbling, but neither Lynne nor Officer Lanur stopped me.

"Okay," Officer Lanur said slowly. I could tell he was having trouble letting go of some little fantasy about effortlessly rescuing two helpless teenage girls from certain death. "Um, is it a mechanical thing? How do we get around this?"

"I don't know," I snapped in frustration.

Lynne was prying at all sides of the window frame with her fingernails, as if she could dig her way out. Tears blurred my eyes as I watched her. I was so tired all of a sudden.

Officer Lanur began talking quietly into a headset I hadn't even noticed he was wearing.

"Um, I'm going to go back up to the roof here for a few minutes," he told us. "I'll bring back some tools to break in without making any noise. I'm sure we'll have you out of there in no time at all." I wondered if that was a white lie, the same kind that police officers told all the time in the movies—like, *Yes, yes, of course you'll live. You'll be fine*, to a person who was obviously bleeding to death.

We watched Officer Lanur rise and disappear over the edge of the roof. Lynne sank down to the floor and slumped against the wall.

"I thought we were getting out," she moaned.

"We've got hours," I said comfortingly. "It'll be a long time before Mom gets here."

Secretly, I was almost relieved that Officer Lanur hadn't been able to rescue us right away. It gave me time to think. Should I refuse to escape without Mom? I could get the police to give me another laptop computer to fool Rona with once

Mom got here. I could tell the police to save Mom first. It couldn't be that difficult, could it?

My thoughts got so convoluted, I didn't hear the phone the first time it rang. But Lynne did.

"Listen," she hissed.

We crawled over to the door. I put my ear against the wood.

"Do you think that's safe?" Lynne asked. She pointed. The bullet hole was only a few inches over my head.

"Shh," I hissed. I peeked out the bullet hole. I could just barely see Rona. "She doesn't have the gun aimed over here," I reassured Lynne. "She's talking on her cell phone."

Rona walked out of my line of vision. I heard her shout, "No!" Then there was a gunshot.

Lynne and I both dived back into the bathtub so quickly, we rocked it on its claw feet.

Outside our room, I could hear Rona shouting, but my ears were still echoing with the gunfire. I couldn't make out the words. Then there were more gunshots. Lynne and I cowered in the bathtub like scared little puppies. I think one of us was crying, but I wasn't even sure if it was her or me.

We heard sirens, the crackle of walkie-talkies, trampling footsteps outside our door. Still, Lynne and I huddled together, without moving, our hands over our heads.

Then we heard a knock on the door.

"Kira? Lynne? Are you all right in there?" It was Officer Lanur. "I think we've found a way around the window problem. You're safe now. Come on out."

Forty-One

IT WAS A LONG TIME BEFORE THE POLICE TOLD US THAT Rona and Jacques were dead. I think they thought we were in shock.

Maybe we were.

Lynne's parents arrived immediately and fell all over her with hugs and kisses and repeated questions: "Are you all right? What happened? Where have you been? Oh, we were so worried!" Her mother clutched Lynne's right hand and her father clutched her left hand, and I could tell that none of them wanted to let go, ever.

I sat alone.

Lynne's mom reached over to me, when she remembered, but I shook my head.

"No," I said. "Stay with Lynne."

We were in my bedroom, where no one had stepped foot since the night before. That's because the rest of the apartment was a crime scene. I walked out into the living room, where Officer Lanur was taking pictures of bullet holes in the wall.

"Have you found my mother yet?" I asked. "They were flying her here. She would have left California, oh, about—" I looked at the clock, but I couldn't make sense of it. I had no idea what time it had been when Rona called Crythe, what time Lynne and I had locked ourselves in the bathroom, what time it was now. Both hands of the clock hung strangely. I hadn't had such trouble telling time since I was in first grade.

Oh. Someone had shot the clock, too.

"Your mom?" Officer Lanur said, as if he had forgotten there was anyone else involved. "We've got the FAA checking out that one. We should be getting word on her location any minute now."

I looked around the room. Blood stained the carpet and the walls. *That will never come out,* I thought. We'd have to replace the carpet and the wallpaper. But that wouldn't be enough to erase what had happened here. The image would stay in my mind forever.

"Why didn't you just get a crowbar?" I asked in a choked voice. "You could have gotten us out the window. You didn't have to come in shooting."

Officer Lanur gave me a hard look.

"The woman—Rona?—she shot the old man," he said. "Right after the phone call. We just came in to defend him, to protect you. But she wouldn't stand down. She just kept shooting and shooting and shooting."

I think maybe Officer Lanur was in shock too. He probably wasn't used to doing anything more dangerous than getting cats out of trees.

"Why?" I asked. "Why'd she shoot him?"

Officer Lanur shrugged. "She was shouting something at the old man, but none of us could understand. It's all on tape. So's the phone call, but it's in some strange language. We'll have to have it interpreted."

"It's Crythian," I said. "I can interpret for you."

He probably shouldn't have given me the tape. A big-city cop would probably have ordered me out of the crime scene, sent me safely into counseling, gone to a professional interpreter who had no emotional involvement. But Officer Lanur went over to the kitchen table and tossed a tape recorder into my hands.

I hit the rewind button.

The police had begun intercepting Rona's phone signals when she called Crythe to ask for Mom to be flown here. I listened to that call impatiently, pushing fast-forward every few seconds. And then I heard a new voice, someone tripping over his words in excitement or horror or fear.

I gasped. I dropped the tape recorder.

Officer Lanur looked back at me, then rushed to my side. He grabbed my shoulders and shook me.

"Kira! Kira!" he shouted. "Talk to me! What is it?"

His voice seemed to come from farther away than California.

I whispered back, and my voice sounded far away too, as if it belonged to somebody else. Or as if I were a ventriloquist, throwing my voice miles away.

"Mom's plane," I said. "It crashed."

Forty-Two

I MOVED IN WITH LYNNE'S FAMILY THAT NIGHT. I'D never known it, but Mom had made arrangements, years ago, for Mr. and Mrs. Robertson to be my guardians if anything ever happened to her.

That was good.

Lynne's parents remind me to do my homework. They pack my lunches. They do my laundry. They tell me to shut up when I protest, "I hope I'm not imposing on you too much..."

"Come on, Kira," Lynne teased one of those times. "What's the difference? You practically lived over here, anyhow, before."

And then we were all uncomfortable, remembering.

Lynne's parents also take me to see Mom, once a week, without fail, every Sunday.

She lies in a hospital bed—barely moving, never speaking.

It's a mental hospital, now.

"Head injuries are strange," the doctor tells me. "Medically speaking, there's no reason for her to be so . . . nonresponsive." He isn't quite willing to use the word "comatose." She doesn't fit any of their usual classifications. "Of course, the CT scans do show some anomalies I've never seen before in any other patient. . . ."

It's the hidden computer port that confuses him. That and all the other tampering my parents did in my mother's mind. He doesn't believe me when I say her brain was highly unusual even before the crash. He keeps speculating about some sort of operation.

"Maybe that's the solution," he says, every time we talk. "If I bring in some specialists . . ."

I'm not sure how much longer the Robertsons can hold him off.

That's why I am glad to be sixteen now, glad to have my driver's license. Glad to have a car sitting in the garage, waiting.

It is spring again now. As soon as school is out—tomorrow—Lynne and I are going on a trip.

First we will kidnap Mom. Oh, we'll sign her out—everything will be official and documented. We're not going to be fugitives from the law or anything like that. The Robertsons will tell the doctors that she's going to have highly qualified, specialized medical care at another facility. But the doctors wouldn't approve if they knew what we were really doing.

Because *I'm* the highly qualified, specialized medical care. The special facility is Mom's car. And we'll be driving cross-country, all the way to Crythe.

No one is living there now. Those who plotted with Rona are all in jail. Everyone else is dead and gone or, like Mom, in mental institutions.

It turns out that Mom and I own the entire village.

That does not concern me.

What I want to do is to take Mom up a certain flight of stairs, to a certain windowless room with stone walls and a pine floor. We will sit there on the floor, just her and me. And I will tell her a story. I will tell her everything I remember. And then I will give her a choice.

It is time to come back to the world, I will tell her. *Who do you want to come back as? Toria or Sophia?*

And then I hope she will find a way to give me an answer. Because I have a laptop I rebuilt, from plans I know by heart. I have computer disks filled with all the memories she might want to keep. I have everything I need to bring her back, except her decision.

Rona told me a lot of lies, but she also told me

one thing that feels like the truth: You are what you remember.

Does Mom want to remember being the bystander, the little sister, the victim? Or does she want to remember being the one who feels responsible, the one who takes the blame?

Last night at twilight, when I was supposed to be at the library studying for my history final (what a joke), I walked over to Maple Street and the house where Mom and I had lived. I sat under the willow tree in the backyard and stared up at the windows for a long time. You might say I was seeing ghosts: thirteen years of me with Mom, going in and out, eating meals, talking together. Growing up. I saw Rona arriving, luring me away. Then I saw Rona, Jacques, Lynne, and me coming back, my head full of dangerous plans. And I saw bullets flying, police swarming, Rona and Jacques dying.

I didn't see dark windows, hiding nothing, until I heard a rustle in the grass.

"Hey," a voice called. "What is this? Hide-and-seek?"

Lynne.

"Did you ever think," I said, "about how I've got to make the same decision as Mom?"

Lynne sat down on the grass beside me. Willow branches reached down to both of us.

"How do you figure that?" she asked.

"I used to think that as soon as Mom was cured, I'd ask you or her to hypnotize me, make me forget everything my parents knew. Go back to being myself. I'd be like Mom was as Sophia. Safe. Protected. Normal."

"Stupid," Lynne chimed in jokingly.

I frowned.

"It's not about intelligence," I protested. "It's more . . . responsibility. Am I responsible for Rona's and Jacques's deaths? Am I responsible for Mom's plane crashing? Am I responsible for the last remaining Crythians? Am I responsible for all the secrets I know?"

Lynne picked a blade of grass and peeled it down to its veins.

"It's not your fault Rona was a trigger-happy lunatic," she said. "It's not your fault Jacques was so desperate to regain his memories after his stroke that he went along with her crazy plot. It's not your fault Jacques's old flying buddy couldn't even take off without crashing."

Somehow I couldn't absolve myself so easily.

I thought about how Rona had gone to the trouble of learning Crythian, of studying Crythian customs, of mastering Crythian memory techniques during the thirteen years after the war in Crythe. Lynne and I had talked about this before—Lynne couldn't dredge up a single shred of understanding for anything Rona had done. But I had my parents' minds in mine. I knew Rona better. I knew more about evil. Now that Rona was safely dead, I could wonder: *Had* she just wanted money? Or, before she went off the deep end, had she found some sense of belonging in Crythe and Crythian myth?

I wasn't sure. Maybe I was just trying to make myself feel better about being fooled by her original act.

It was easier to think about Jacques. Jacques was just a pitiful old man. I could feel sad about him dying.

"Maybe if I'd come up with a different plan," I said to Lynne. "Some other way to keep you and Mom and me safe—"

"You did the best you could," Lynne said. "You didn't know everything that was going to happen. Even your brilliant parents couldn't foresee the future."

She was teasing again. It's funny how Lynne used to be the one who was always too serious. She broke off another blade of grass to dissect.

"You know what?" she said. "I bet even if you wanted to stick your head in the sand, forget about your parents' invention, you couldn't. You've used those memories. They're part of your mind now."

Sometimes, even now, Lynne can still seem smarter than me. I shook my head, wanting to deny everything.

"What scares me," I said, "is that I was ready to zap Rona's memories. That's what I was going to do at the end, when Mom was safe with us." Lynne knew this, but it seemed important to tell her again. "I was going to trick Rona into exchanging her memories for those of some harmless old Crythian. And that would have been wrong. That would have been using their invention for my own personal gain."

Lynne punched my shoulder. I think she meant it playfully, but it didn't feel playful.

"You idiot, don't be so hard on yourself. You were just trying to stay alive. To keep your mom and me alive."

I stared up at the dark windows and blinked quickly, so Lynne wouldn't see that I was crying. That's all the Crythians were doing too—trying to stay alive through their memories, their memorizations, their Aunt Memory trainings, their endless, obsessive attention to every small detail of life. I have all that in me, but I have Willistown, too, and careless Friday-night sleepovers where we watch stupid movies that we all but forget by Monday morning. And I have friends who care about *me*, not just the convoluted secrets in my mind.

My eyes blurred, and I saw something on the steps of my old apartment that was not a memory. I saw Mom and me coming back from Crythe together. We had our arms around each other's waists and our heads were bent together, talking. In this vision of the future I couldn't tell if she had decided to return to consciousness as Sophia or Toria or, somehow, both at once. I couldn't tell what I had decided about my parents' memories either. Or my parents' invention. But we were happy.

The Crythian motto was wrong. I am not just what I remember. I am also what I dream.

Imagine a world where families are allowed only two children.

Illegal third children—shadow children—must live in hiding,

for if they are discovered, there is only one punishment:

Death.

Read the Shadow Children series by

MARGARET PETERSON HADDIX

Looking for a great read?

MARGARET PETERSON HADDIX

MARS HAS A MILLION DIFFERENT WAYS TO KILL YOU. . . .

The year is 2085. Mars Experimental Station One, a colony built to test humans' ability to live in an alien and hostile environment, has been in existence for ten years. This functioning city of two thousand people includes only twenty teenagers, each hand selected from the billions on Earth as part of the controversial Asimov Project.

The Asimov teens each have reasons to doubt themselves and distrust each other. But one thing is certain: Mars offers them something Earth never could. When the existence of Marsport is threatened, the group must overcome their fears and join forces, for their survival depends on nothing less.

FOLLOW THE ADVENTURES OF THESE TEENS IN THE MARS YEAR ONE TRILOGY:

#1 MAROONED!
#2 MISSING!
#3 MARSQUAKE!

ALADDIN PAPERBACKS
SIMON & SCHUSTER CHILDREN'S DIVISION

PENDRAGON

Bobby Pendragon is a seemingly normal fourteen-year-old boy. He has a family, a home, and a possible new girlfriend. But something happens to Bobby that changes his life forever.

HE IS CHOSEN TO DETERMINE
THE COURSE OF HUMAN EXISTENCE.

Pulled away from the comfort of his family and suburban home, Bobby is launched into the middle of an immense, interdimensional conflict involving racial tensions, threatened ecosystems, and more. It's a journey of danger and discovery for Bobby, and his success or failure will do nothing less than determine the fate of the world. . . .

PENDRAGON

by D. J. MacHale

Book One: The Merchant of Death
Book Two: The Lost City of Faar
Book Three: The Never War
Book Four: The Reality Bug
Book Five: Black Water

Coming Soon: Book Six: The Rivers of Zadaa

From Aladdin Paperbacks • Published by Simon & Schuster

OUTCAST

#1 The Un-Magician
by Christopher Golden & Thomas E. Sniegoski

TIMOTHY IS A FREAK, a weakling, an impossibility. He's the only person in existence without magical powers and has spent his entire life hidden on a remote island.

When Timothy is finally taken back to the city of his birth, he finds he is marked for death. Assassins are watching his every move, and the government wants him destroyed. Timothy can't imagine what threat he could possibly pose; after all, he wields no power in this world.

Or does he?

The OutCast quartet begins August 2004

Aladdin Paperbacks • Simon & Schuster Children's Publishing Division
www.simonsayskids.com